ALL THE
fine ass dopemen

NASTEE

contents

Stormeisha (Black Girl Tired BookTok)
Jazzy (The BookTok Rookie)
Shaunee (AudreyShanice)
Bewticious (B. Bewtie)
Shanny (BIH_IREADBOOKS)
Dosey-Dose (DoseofQ)
Lil' Baby AKA Jack-Jack (Resourcefulbooks)
Tash AKA Twinny (Tashtheauthor)
Arie My Personal Thelma
Joshua Matthews (Our only Tiktok Brother, lol)

The ENTIRE Boozy Book Baddies Community
BookTok
My Facebook Group: The Reading Chamber
Bookstagrammers
To everyone who read book 1, left a review, made
a video… I LOVE YOUUUUU.

Momo7reads
Jazz_itupabit
Aamriyaaareads
Honeymelaninandlocs
Booksnlocs90

Chardonnaysbooknook
Shalaundascorners
Officiallytylee918
Kserf98
Royalcrown336
Bookedandbizzie
Naturaallyfearless
Charny86
Nellie_1989
Bookgirlom iranda
Coco_readsspicy
Shesnaturallydope87
Tonireads_1
Bookplugjessica
Kireyaboo
Latoya Watts

Now listen y'all, you know this was a re-release. There has been slight content added for your reading pleasure. It was formerly known as another book now titled All The Fine Ass Dope Men.

This is the finale of the original series, but there is more to come. Also, I don't want no confusion when you see the cliffhanger from book 2 as a chapter here. Because it was in the last book as a reminder. Also, when y'all say things like "it's too much goin' on" in a review and leave a 2-3 star and then come read the next book, y'all just as wild and toxic as me! Slide out for me!

TWENTY-SIX YEARS AGO...

"*Can I get you something, baby, before the meeting?*" *Jayla asked Juaqeen as she wobbled through the conference room of their home. Jayla was eight months pregnant with Cocaine, and even though she could barely stand up on her own two feet, she always made sure to prepare food and an assortment of refreshments for Juaqeen's business meetings.*

"No, my love. I'm good. You go ahead and go rest. I'll bring you something to snack on a little bit later. You know the doctor said you're not supposed to be up moving around like this. Give me a kiss and go get settled."

Jayla smiled and rubbed her belly. She was blessed with the honor of carrying the most precious bundle of joy in the world, her sweet baby, Cocaine. Jayla leaned over and kissed Juaqeen, passionately on the lips, sticking her tongue deep into his throat, just the way he liked.

Juaqeen pulled away from her. She had a way of turning him on like no other woman had ever, and he didn't need a hard brick in his pants before his meeting.

"Hey, boss, Amir is here to see you," Leon said as he opened the door to the conference room.

Jayla ran her hands over her yellow sun flowered dress that was now raising up due to her pregnant belly and swollen ass.

Amir walked in with his head held high. His wrists and hands illuminated in gold. As soon as Juaqeen laid eyes on him, he felt uneasy. He'd heard about the way Amir did business, and he wasn't in the habit of doing business with people like Amir, but he was a professional, and above all, he was a real nigga. He figured every person deserved the respect of being told to their face that they were being rejected. Besides, he knew once he gave Amir the bad news, there might be some type of retaliation, even if it was a small one, and Juaqeen preferred to know his enemies by face and name.

Juaqeen kissed Jayla on the cheek, and Leon held the door for her. As Amir continued walking in, he took notice of the pregnant woman and was taken by her beauty. The glow around her could have been from pregnancy, but he was positive it came from her over all essence.

"Juaqeen, thank you for seeing me on such short notice." Amir extended his hand, and Juaqeen met it for a firm shake.

"It's no problem, why don't you have a seat."

The gentlemen took a seat at the table, and Juaqeen wanted to get straight into it.

"So, Amir, I've looked over everything, asked around, and I'ma just be honest with you because I prefer to be honest so that I can receive the same in return. I'm not in the habit of doing business with desperate men. I know you're desperate because you've taken meetings with not only me, but others in even lower circles, which tells me you'll take help from anyone who's offering it, and that can be dangerous, so unfortunately, I'm going to have to decline your offer."

Amir couldn't believe this. He'd come all the way from a different state to hear bad news? He could've been told this over the phone, in a letter, anything, but coming all the way down here was not necessary.

"Well, I'm not sure what to say. I'm not a desperate man in the terms of money, but I'm sure you know, I'm about to go to war with a neighboring gang, my drug supply has dwindled down to almost nothing, so I do need help. I'm desperate for time, not necessarily for money. I need resources. I'm not above asking for that either."

"While I appreciate your honesty, I'm still not interested. I have a family to think about. I have a son on the way, plans being made, I'm down here fighting a war myself, so I just don't think it's time for me to be getting engaged in someone else's affairs, especially when they have nothing to offer me in exchange."

Amir slapped his fists on the table and stood up.

"I'm offering you a chance at expansion, the opportunity to join forces with my team. We have some of the best soldiers in the world, and I feel confident enough to say that. You might want to rethink your decision. Saying no to me may not prove to be in your favor."

Juaqeen rose from his chair and looked him in the eye. "Are you threatening me, or making a lame attempt at it?"

"I don't threaten, this is a promise. I'll give you a few days to think about it, and then you can get back to—"

"Trust me, it ain't nothin' to think about. I'm good on you. Leon, come show this clown to the fuckin' door, now!"

Leon, who was just standing on the other side of the door, pushed the door open and rose his hand in the direction of the front room.

Amir smiled a devilish smile and wiped his chin. Juaqeen didn't know it, but this would be the meeting to open a string of bad things happening to him. From this moment forward, his life would slowly fall apart, but he wouldn't find that out for years to come.

After Amir was gone, as he promised, Juaqeen went upstairs to join Jayla. He had the chef fix her favorite meal, hashbrown casserole, a sausage and cheese omelet, and biscuits and gravy. Jayla could smell the food before Juaqeen even came in the room. As soon as he turned the corner, she sat up on the bed and licked her lips. She didn't know which looked better, her man or the food.

"As promised, my lady. I got you some food."

Juaqeen sat the food on the bed in front of her, slid out of his shoes and his clothes, stripping all the way down to his boxers, and he slid into bed next to her.

"Thank you, baby. You want some?"

"Nah, not right now. You go ahead."

That was all Jayla needed to hear. She was more than ready to dig in. As she ate her food, she couldn't help but notice Juaqeen who was staring her plate down. With a mouth full of food, stuffed to capacity, she slowly turned her head to the side and jumped at him.

"What?" she asked, food garbling around in her cheeks.

"I was gon' see if I could get some of that now."

"Oh, so you wanna wait till I got a whole rhythm going to get some. Get out of here. You should've gotten it while the getting was still hot."

Jayla pulled her elbows up, guarding her food so Juaqeen wouldn't try to get any.

"Damn, stingy, fat ass. Go ahead on then. I ain't want none anyway."

Juaqeen folded his arms and watched her finish eating. He didn't give a shit for real. He was just happy that she was happy and that she was eating. The last few weeks had been hard on Jayla. She didn't have much of an appetite, and she was tired all the time, which the doctor said was normal for this time in her pregnancy, and when she was hungry, she was starving, ravenous even, so Juaqeen made sure he kept her well fed, fucked, and happy. The sex was more for him than it was for her though, of course.

Jayla finished her food and sat her plate on the end table next to her.

"Now that your big, hungry-hungy hippo ass is done eating, I figured we could watch a movie. What you wanna see?"

Jayla loved movie night with Juaqeen. He always chose the best movies, and he never went back on a move night. If he said they were going to watch a movie, they did just that. He would put the house on complete lockdown so they could enjoy their evening together.

"Whatever you pick is what we'll watch."

Juaqeen and Jayla had a very extensive VHS collection, and since Jayla was comfy in bed, she let Juaqeen go ahead and pick the movie; he was better at it than her anyway.

After he selected the movie, he set the TV up and went downstairs to get some snacks. As he was popping the popcorn on the stove, he heard something coming from upstairs, but he had no clue what it was.

Juaqeen got Leon to watch the stove, and he headed upstairs to see what was going on.

When he opened the door to his bedroom, Jayla was leaned over with her hand on her stomach, rubbing it over and over again. Her head was almost in between her legs she was leaned over so far.

"Baby, what's wrong?" Juaqeen asked as he rushed to her side.

Jayla looked up with tears in her eyes, and then down on the floor. Between her legs was a giant wet spot with little red droplets mixed in with it.

"I think it's time, baby," Jayla said to Juaqeen through broken *words. She was so excited to finally be having Cocaine. She couldn't wait to see him, and finally, their family would be complete. Juaqeen and Jayla weren't married, but he'd planned to ask her just before she told him she was pregnant, but he knew the way she thought, and if he would've asked then, she would have thought it was because she was telling him she was pregnant, when that wasn't the case at all. Juaqeen truly loved him some Jayla, and though it had taken her some time to realize it, she saw it, and she felt it.*

Juaqeen didn't want to waste any time. When he came around the bed and saw the blood, his mind instinctively pushed itself to protection mode, and he would do anything and everything he possibly could to make sure Jayla had a safe delivery.

Though the doctors hadn't plain come out and said it, they'd hinted to Jayla possibly having a difficult birth. Jayla's small frame had made it almost impossible for her to carry a ten-pound baby, but she had done it successfully, but in truth, she was ready to get this baby out of her.

"Come on, baby." Juaqeen scooped her up in his arms as she wrapped hers around his neck, and he carried her downstairs.

"Should I make the announcement, Juaqeen?" Leon asked.

The whole hood was waiting on this moment. Cocaine was a prince amongst the people, and most of them couldn't wait to see him and shower him with love and presents, but there was always of course someone lurking, waiting to destroy something amazing.

Leon grabbed the baby bag they'd been putting together over the last few months that Jayla would need when they got to the hospital, he placed it in the back of the car, and he wished the couple well.

No one was more excited than Leon. He couldn't wait to meet Cocaine. They'd never had a baby in the house, so he couldn't wait to see how such a small person could disrupt the natural flow of things, and he looked forward to Juaqeen being at home much more.

After closing the door behind Juaqeen and Jayla, Leon began making his phone calls to the leaders in the hood. Juaqeen didn't know it, but they had been organizing a party behind his back, a secret baby shower, but Jayla was giving birth a lot earlier than they'd planned, so the party wouldn't be happening, but that didn't mean they couldn't bring the gifts to them.

As Leon made the phone calls, the word began to spread like wildfire that Cocaine was about to make his grand entry into the world, and in doing so, this information fell into the wrong hands, Amir.

Juaqeen was right; he was so desperate he would do business with anyone he saw fit, including the enemy of an enemy. Though the streets loved Juaqeen for his hard work and dedication to the community, he had rivals that didn't want to see him succeed, and because of this, he made enemies, enemies who would stop at nothing to see the end of the Blackwood line come into fruition.

Larry "Big Dog" Hodeson was one of Juaqeen's many enemies, and once he heard the news of the baby who would be born, and of course would eventually take over, he and his crew knew it was time to start making moves against him. Slowly, they'd been making noise here and there, robbing trap spots, killing Juaqeen's soldiers, trying to get noticed, but this, this would take the cake.

Amir and Larry had just shaken on an agreement when Larry got the call about Juaqeen's son who was about to be born. Amir had expressed his anger once Larry agreed to help him about Juaqeen turning him down, so he knew Amir would be eager to help. The plan was to get the baby and raise him as their own, as a part of the Ninth Ward's Kings, but Amir wasn't into kidnapping children. He instead had his own plan and would exact his revenge tonight.

Amir, who was almost untainted before this situation, was always just a breath away from falling off his rocker, due to a mental disease that was beyond his control, since he refused to take his meds, and it altered his reality and sense of right and wrong.

Amir didn't have a family of his own just yet, but he knew that when he did, he would do everything he could for them. For now, while he was by himself, he wanted to make enough money and stability to be able to give to the children he might have in the future. Though Amir had many women, he wasn't stupid enough to nut in them because he knew he didn't have the time nor finances to necessarily be there for them just yet, so he would wait until he could.

Money and stability were the motive, and Amir was willing to go way, way too far to make that dream a reality.

Juaqeen and Jayla made it to the hospital in just enough time. By the time Jayla made it to the delivery room, Cocaine's head was already sliding out of her vagina, so they had to work quickly to get Cocaine out of there safely.

Before Jayla was even rushed to the back, Juaqeen said he couldn't stand to be in the room. He'd seen dead bodies, even killed his own fair share of people, but he saw the birth video when Jayla first told him she was pregnant because she wanted to have a natural birth with no medication, but Juaqeen wanted to know what all that entailed, and in doing so, it blew his mind and completely fucked him up. He knew he wasn't going to be able to go in the delivery room with her because seeing her be ripped apart like that was not something he could stomach; even seeing her in pain in the car was fucking with him, and he couldn't take it.

Before they pushed her to the back, he leaned over her and kissed her, deeply.

"I love you, Jayla, and when we leave this hospital, I'ma give you my last name. I mean it."

Jayla raised her hand and placed it across his heart. "I love you too, Juaqeen. Now let me go, I gotta go give birth to our future."

Juaqeen smiled. This was the best day of his life, and this day was all he could've imagined.

***

"Ok, Jayla, we need you to push. Take a deep breath, and push!" the doctor coached her through the first push. Jayla was now wishing she'd taken the Lamaze classes her mother and sister told her about, who she was sure was in the waiting room by now, probably giving Juaqeen a hard time. They didn't like him at all, and they wanted Jayla to dump him because of all of his street dealings, but Jayla wouldn't leave him for all the world, no matter what anyone said.

As Jayla pushed, her thoughts were on Juaqeen. She thought about how proud he would be of her that she gave him the greatest gift of all, and she couldn't wait to celebrate that love together.

Jayla continued following the doctor's orders, looking into the mirror that reflected from her feet to the mirror beside her, something she'd requested so she could actually see the moment the baby was born.

Several pushes later, Cocaine was sliding out like a well buttered turkey coming out of the oven.

"Waa-waa!" Cocaine's cries could be heard throughout the delivery room.

"Let me see him," Jayla said as she held her arms open to receive her baby. The nurse placed a wrapped up, half wiped off Cocaine into her arms, and Jayla's heart had never been more open. Everything she'd ever done wrong in her life, or even right at this point didn't even matter. Cocaine was the most important thing in the world to her, and he was her greatest accomplishment.

Clap! Clap! Clap!

Jayla's moment with Cocaine was broken due to the sound of a very loud clapping sound. The nurse removed Cocaine from her hands and took him out of the delivery room to take him to the nursery to be where all babies go once they're born.

"Good job, doc. Congratulations, Jayla on having your first born."

A man who was dressed in scrubs and a white mask began disrobing himself.

"Uhm, excuse me, you can't be in here," Jayla's doctor, Doctor Domm said as he stepped closer to the man who was taking his clothes off.

"I wouldn't get too close if I were you, doc," Amir said as he removed his gun from the waistband in his clothes. His scrubs were now off, and everyone in the room could see his face.

"What are you doing in here?" Jayla asked. She remembered the man from earlier that day in her home.

"Simple. Doc, don't you move, tell ya' little nurses to get over there too by the counter. Now, this is how this is gon' go. Jayla's coming with me. Don't worry, I ain't gon' kill her; I just wanna get even with Juaqeen. He wasted my time, and now, I'm going to waste his."

"Sir, I can't let you do that. She just had a baby. She can't just leave with you."

"Sure she can. I've already made arrangements for her to leave in a day or so, and don't think I won't kill you if you try to alarm somebody, so here's what you gon' do. Y'all are gonna give her somethin' to put her ass in a coma or some shit where she appears to be dead to other people. Ain't nobody got time to be goin' through no bullshit. It's gotta be believable, and in return, you'll all be paid handsomely. Y'all were in the right delivery room today!"

Amir was being very cocky, another reason why Juaqeen didn't want to do business with him. He could tell by the way he'd been acting that day that he was full of himself, and Juaqeen's personality was big enough for all of them; he didn't need another ego mixed with his.

Jayla, who was just a few seconds from passing out from all the blood she'd lost, was able to mutter just a few words before completely being rendered unconscious. "If you think…you can get away with this…you don't know Juaqeen, so do what you gotta do, but this won't go that far."

Jayla's heart rate dropped, and she was going into critical condition.

"If you want to be able to take her anywhere, you'll need to let me help her now before there is no one to take," Doctor Domm said in a shaky tone.

He had to seal up the hole that ripped between Jayla's vagina and butt hole and stop the bleeding that was caused when she gave birth.

The nurses surrounded the doctor and helped him assist Jayla. Amir flashed the money he had for all of them, and unfortunately, money truly is the root of all evil. It could change even the best people and make them do things they might not normally do.

The doctors and nurses worked effortlessly to put her back together, and Doctor Domm administered Jayla a drug that would place her into a coma like state to make her seem like she was gone.

When Juaqeen found out about Jayla passing away, he was heartbroken, and a part of him didn't want to believe it.

Though Jayla lie lifeless on the table, Juaqeen couldn't believe his son's mother was gone. The love of his life was gone. Juaqeen held Cocaine in his arms and leaned him down to see his mother. He knew Cocaine wouldn't understand what was going on, but he hoped he would have some type of recollection of who this person was eventually.

The day Jayla was "buried," the casket was closed. The doctors told her family that it would be best because of all the "swelling" she'd endured after giving birth from the medicine, and like idiots, they believed it. Truly, her mother and father both believed this was the fate she suffered because she chose to be with Jaqueen. She'd gone against their wishes, and now, their daughter had paid the price.

The doctor was also a family friend. Not to mention, Amir paid off the funeral home to keep the secret and keep it quiet. No one knew who was truly going into that box; it was a regular Jane Doe, someone from the morgue who hadn't been claimed.

Amir moved Jayla while she was still in an unconscious state back to Tennessee, where he would keep her prisoner for well over twenty years….

J uaqeen kicked the cage, repeatedly with all of his strength. After all of these years, he couldn't believe she was alive. He'd always hoped that somehow, she was, but he didn't know if it was possible or if it was all in his mind—something he'd made up. This was terrifyingly beautiful.

When the cage wouldn't open, Juaqeen snatched the gun away from his father and told Jayla to stand as far against the other side of the cage as she possibly could.

Jayla, who was discombobulated and completely surprised was so in shock, she didn't hear Juaqeen who was telling her to get back, but Juaqeen didn't have time for that. He had to get her out of there so that Lexxy could get to a hospital. Juaqeen fired the gun, startling Jayla out of whatever daze she was in.

The lock on the cage popped off, and the door opened. Jayla looked as though she wasn't used to personal interaction or any personal attention. The closer Juaqeen got to her, she cowered to the back of the cage, trying to scoot as far away as possible. Though she wanted to scream, her throat was so dry, she couldn't make a peep. Juaqeen reached into the cage and grabbed her gently, trying to help get her out of the cage. When he got a closer look, she was naked from the waist down. Juaqeen couldn't believe the love of his life had been treated so poorly, and he promised himself when the time came, he would kill whoever did this to her. Juaqeen removed his shirt and wrapped it around her waist.

"Come on, baby," Juaqeen whispered as he helped her stand to her feet. She was so skinny, skinnier than she had been when she was healthy. Jayla's two legs were entirely too wobbly, she couldn't stand up on her own. Like the hero he was, Juaqeen picked her up and held her like he had the last time he was with her.

Wild Bill and Lexxy were already in the car, waiting for Roman and Juaqeen to join them. Wild Bill didn't want to start the car as not to bring attention to them until it was time. From the side of the house, Wild Bill could hear Cocaine tussling with who he assumed was Paul and Quentin, but if there was one thing they were all certain of: Cocaine could handle himself.

Roman and Juaqeen came stumbling out of the house with Jayla in Juaqeen's arms. Roman pulled the door open to the large blacked out SUV and helped Juaqeen lay her in the back seat, just in front of Lexxy who was laid out a row behind her.

Lexxy was in so much pain, she didn't have the energy to lean up and see what was going on. Her mind was on her baby and her husband. This entire time, she hadn't seen Cocaine, and she wondered where he was, but she was going in between consciousness and definitive unconsciousness, so she couldn't even ask if she wanted to what was happening.

Though Cocaine and Quentin were supposed to be

having a fair fight, Cocaine was getting the best of him, so Paul had to jump in to rescue his brother. Several punches to the face, head, and ribs had left Quentin not only bloody but with broken and bruised ribs, not to mention the fact that Cocaine had kicked them in both of their chins, so they were sore all over and were having a problem regaining control over the fight, and that fact alone pissed Paul off. He was tasked with the same charge most older siblings are: protection, and he felt like he had failed to do so. It didn't help any that it had begun raining.

As sweat and rain mixed, clouding the three men's vision, dripping down their faces, Paul grew tired of seeing his brother get his ass whooped, and there was only one thing he knew to do. Sure, Quentin had said he was going to play by the rules and fight like a man, but Paul never agreed to such bullshit.

Paul pulled his gun from his backside and pulled the hammer back, popping Cocaine right in the rib.

"Shit!" Cocaine yelled as he stumbled backwards.

Hearing the gunshot and with the car finally being loaded, Wild Bill was in the middle row, Juaqeen was in the front, Jayla and Lexxy in both of the back rows, and Roman driving, the SUV pulled up to the front of the house. Juaqeen hoped for Paul and Quentin's sake that one of them had been shot, but when they reached the front of the house, Juaqeen saw Cocaine on the ground, and he lost it. This day was already stressful enough. None of them had any rest, their minds were going haywire, and now, his emotions had been played on with Jayla, and his son was the icing on the cake.

Juaqeen jumped out of the passenger seat with the gun he'd snatched from Roman, pointing it at Paul as he moved to shield Cocaine from Paul possibly finishing the job. Juaqeen was prepared to shoot, but he was frozen by the words that were shouted in his direction.

"Don't! Don't shoot my son! Please, don't shoot!"

Those words were undeniable. There was no way Juaqeen could have mistaken them. He turned around, along with everyone else to face the shouting woman who was hanging out of the door.

"Wha—what did you just say?" Juaqeen asked as he stared at her, wondering how something like this could be true.

"Those are my children, please…don—" Jayla couldn't finish her sentence. She fell out of the open door, and Juaqeen couldn't even move to save her from falling. Cocaine saw the woman who had fallen out and onto the ground, but there was no way she was who he thought she was. How in the hell could she be alive after all this time? Though Cocaine had been happy to see his father and was still a bit confused, this was something new. This was some shit that was unheard of. None of the people in his life knew how to stay dead, not that that was what he wanted, but he was used to them being gone. T, well he just wasn't used to.

Paul and Quentin were looking just as surprised. This woman, who had been in the basement of the abandoned home they'd overseen for years, was their mother? How could this be? This goes to show what happens when you do what your parents tell you to do without asking any questions. Sometimes loyalty can result in consequences unforeseen, like this.

If this was true, Cocaine, Quentin, and Paul were brothers, half-brothers, but brothers nonetheless.

Juaqeen finally snapped his mind back into reality. He helped Jayla back in the car and then ran out and got Cocaine who was holding his ribs that had completely gone numb.

Cocaine limped to the car with his father holding onto him. The trunk popped, and Cocaine climbed in the back, looking over the seat at Lexxy who was passed out. He moved the hair out of her beautiful face, taking a good look at her, and he promised he'd kill Paul and Quentin for doing this to her. She looked to be in pain, and the blood and wet spots between her legs let him know she was.

Before Cocaine lie down, he tried to process what happened, but there just wasn't enough time in the damn world to accept the fact that his grandfather, father, and his own mother were back in his life, and she was the mother of the two hellions who were trying to take him and his family out.

Roman had been sitting back watching too much happen. He was used to shooting first and never asking questions. He didn't give a damn about these boys being Jayla's kids; they were of no direct relation to him, and they were trying to kill his grandson and kidnapped his grandson's wife. These niggas had it coming.

Roman rolled the window down on Juaqeen's side and grabbed the gun from Juaqeen. It had been a long time since he had to bust and really get gully on a nigga, but that didn't mean he didn't remember how or didn't still enjoy it. He began firing shots back to back, maneuvering the car in different positions as he shot out the window. Quentin and Paul scurried back into the house, trying to get out of the line of fire.

"Dad! Damn, ok. Stop, we need to get to the hospital now! Jayla, Lexxy, and Cocaine are all down. You need to just turn the car around and hit the highway towards the hospital. Wild Bill, you got us on the directions?"

"Yeah, turn around and bust this left!"

As they rode to the hospital, Juaqeen had a million questions running through his mind. He mainly wondered how something like this could've happened, how all of this time had passed and there were so many things he didn't know and didn't understand.

He'd stayed away from Cocaine to make sure everything was safe, considering he'd been fighting a drug war with his father in Haiti, and he didn't want to bring that noise to his son in anyway, and as soon as he comes back into his life, there was more drama. Juaqeen expected there to be something going on, after all, Cocaine was a Blackwood, and if he was anything like his father or grandfather, trouble followed him wherever he went, but this was more than trouble. This was full out warfare.

Now Juaqeen wondered if staying away from Cocaine would've helped. He couldn't help but feel like all of this was somehow his fault, like his return was some type of universal karma coming back to smack them all in the face. Though staying away from him had been hard, he always worried about the danger that showing up on his son's doorstep might bring. In reality, none of this was his fault, but it all started because of Dutch. There were so many factors that came into play, so many people involved; there was truly no way of telling who got this shit poppin'. Even though Dutch was the person who shot Juaqeen and THOUGHT he killed him, Amir was the one who really started the string of unfortunate events, but Juaqeen didn't know that.

Though Juaqeen hadn't seen Jayla in years, he never forgot the love of his life. The way her smile could light up the world, the way her voice always sounded like angels were singing directly in his ears, her sacrifice to carry their child. He couldn't forget her, and now, looking at her through a mirror seemed unreal. He'd learned to live without her, as he had his son and his mother, but this, this was enough to knock him out, to take him down.

After all of these years, though Juaqeen still got his rocks off, he never fell for anyone. He'd always kept his heart reserved for Jayla, not in hopes of her coming back, but she was the only woman for him, and his love to potentially give to a woman died with her, or so he thought.

R oman had almost reached the hospital where Lexxy worked when she woke up. She sprang up, looking around, surveying her surroundings. She was in so much pain and looking down reminded her of what happened to her; the blood, the smell, it was putrid. She recognized the road they were on, and there was no way she was going to the hospital she worked in.

"Daddy, we have to go to another hospital. Please, don't take me to Baptist. I'd rather not die tonight if I don't have to, and that's what will happen if you take me there."

Roman looked in the backseat and heard Lexxy speaking. She sounded passionate, almost afraid even.

"If she no wan' go, show me anotha one."

"Baptist is closer than Vandy; you sure you don't wanna go there?" Wild Bill asked as he stared into her eyes.

Lexxy thought about the last few weeks at the hospital and how she'd been seeing Carley more and more. Every time she did, she made it a point to speak to her, to be "nice" to her, but she didn't want to think too much into it. She tried to think the best of people, but the best in people wasn't always available. A lot of times, "the best" was their worst.

Lexxy thought about how Carley got the drop on her. Before she passed out after hitting the wall on the interstate, she remembered hearing voices around her, one of which she was very familiar with at this point; it was Carley's. She was part of the master plan, the one who told Quentin and Paul how to find her. She couldn't help but mention that this was her idea and that she was the one who made this happen.

"Yeah, be careful with her because she's pregnant, but by the time I'm done with her ass, that shit won't even matter," Carley said as they got into the other car and drove away.

When they arrived at the abandoned house, Lexxy had finally woken up, and she already knew what was going on. She wouldn't scream or cry; she wasn't that type, and this wasn't the first time she'd been kidnapped though she was much older this time. When she was a little girl something similar had happened. One of the many men who wanted Dutch's head took Lexxy as she was coming out of school. Though he didn't harm her, he kept her for six days, but Lexxy wasn't afraid then, and she wasn't afraid now.

Quentin carried Lexxy into the dirty, non-powered house with a laugh that Lexxy would never be able to get out of her head. Carley, who was coming in behind them was also laughing, sending chills down Lexxy's back. The only place she'd ever heard that type of crazy laugh was on movies or television shows with villains, and in this case, they were definitely villains. Where the hell was Batman when you needed him?

When they got into the living room, the three of them split up. Quentin carried Lexxy downstairs to the basement where she could smell the stench before she even got in it. She didn't know what they wanted, and she wasn't going to ask. She wouldn't give them the satisfaction of knowing that she had no clue what was going on. Lexxy thought after the wedding that everything was ok, but it apparently wasn't.

Quentin took her down the stairs and waited 'til he got close enough to the bottom, and he tossed her to the ground, sending her tumbling down at least five stairs.

"Now look, you gon' stay down here and be a good girl. You got a little mate over there in the corner, just so you know. Hopefully, your little boyfriend will come to save you, maybe he will, maybe he won't. Doesn't really matter to us. Either way, he'll fall apart, and we'll still have what we want."

"What is it that you want?" Lexxy asked. If she was going to be stuck down here, she wanted to know why. Why she was going to be forced to stay down here with some unknown person that she couldn't even see.

"Easy. We want the gorilla gang, the money—we want everything that belongs to us, and your boyfriend is going to give it to us."

"He's my husband, and good luck on that! I'd rather him let me die than let y'all take over."

Even though Lexxy said that, she knew deep down inside that Cocaine would never let anything happen to her, even if that meant losing everything that was given to them at birth.

Lexxy lie on the ground of the basement, cold, hungry, and irritable. She wished she had it in her to be scared. If anything, she was more worried about what Cocaine would do to get her back than she was of what they were going to do to her.

Though Lexxy wasn't there long, Carley was the one who fed her, though she was rough, and often purposely spilled most of the food on her, at least she got to eat. Carley made sure the food was extra hot an almost nonedible, but Lexxy was thankful she didn't have to have a bowel movement while she was there. It was bad enough that they wouldn't let her go to a toilet to pee, not that there was any electricity or plumbing in the place anyway.

A few hours before Lexxy's rescue, Carley came down to the bottom of the stairs and stared at Lexxy. Though Lexxy was tired, hungry, stinking, and unbelievably dirty, she glared at Carley with a look that rocked her to her core.

"You know, I didn't even do this for Quentin and Paul; I did this for me. I just can't forget how my man, the father of my child was so stuck on you, he thought he was going to leave me and his son to be with you. I couldn't let that happen, and now, every day, I'm constantly wondering if it's gon' be you or the next bitch. See, my brothers, they're idiots. They should've killed you from jump. I wouldn't have even just kept you here if it weren't for them, but I just gotta know, what the fuck is so special about you? Can't be your pussy, so it's gotta be something else."

Lexxy was so tired, and she hadn't been able to really sleep in such a dirty place for the fear of bugs crawling on her, or getting to her brain from her body, but even in her darkest moment, she was able to still piss Carley off.

"Here's what's so special about me, I'm a ride or die bitch. I love my men like I love myself—unconditionally and forever. I'm different because I'm not crazy for no reason, like some people in this room. I guess y'all just kidnap whoever you want, whenever you want. You got somebody in that corner who hasn't spoken this entire time, and any time you go to feed her, she jumps around her cage like a monkey. Y'all are some sick muthafuckas."

Carley smirked, but she didn't like being called sick. She wasn't sick; she did what she had to do, or at least that's what she thought.

Carley rose from the stairs and went over to Lexxy who was propped up against the basement wall. The truth was, she was intimidated by Lexxy. She didn't understand what Lucky was stuck on or how she was able to get such a boss like Cocaine. Cocaine was the type of man she always figured she'd end up with, but she didn't. Instead, she was stuck on her baby daddy, who wasn't really good for shit but some dick and paying bills. But she loved him and couldn't help it.

When she got in front of Lexxy, she admired her strength, but it annoyed her a bit. She wanted her to be afraid of her, to know that she was about to get fucked up, so she began punching her in the face, making her nose bloody, and her face swell the size of a melon, and even then, Lexxy just laughed. She laughed until she couldn't see anymore.

Lexxy wanted to fight her back, but she was tied up, so that wasn't going to happen, no way. Lexxy didn't really care as long as her baby was ok. She'd been feeling strange though since she'd been there. She hadn't felt the baby flutter around in her stomach like a butterfly. She hadn't felt anything, but she figured that was from the stress she was experiencing.

Finally, when Lexxy continued showing no signs of fear or weakness, Carley knew the only thing that would make her scream. All of the nurses had been buzzing around the hospital about Lexxy's pregnancy and how excited they were that she and her husband were able to reproduce after what she'd gone through with the transplant, the doctors were praising her as if it were some sort of miracle, but Carley didn't give a shit. She didn't think it was that big of a deal, but that was just her jealousy speaking, but she knew that would be the only thing that would fuck with her. The only thing to make her go crazy would be having damage done to her baby.

Carley was a nurse, and she knew what to do to damage a pregnant mother, plus, she was smart. She knew that if she kicked her belly with enough blunt force, she'd lose her child, or at least the baby would come out with some type of problem. She was starting to regret feeding her and giving her water because that made her a lot stronger.

With all of her might, Carley began kicking Lexxy over and over, going over and over again until Quentin ran downstairs after hearing the yelling and pulled her off of Lexxy.

"The fuck is wrong with you! She's pregnant. We ain't runnin' around giving homemade abortions. Get yo' stupid ass upstairs." Quentin pulled Carley's arm and forced her up the stairs.

Quentin wanted revenge, true enough, but he wasn't about to let Carley keep on beating Lexxy. That wasn't ok, but he damn sure wasn't going to apologize.

Quentin took a look at Lexxy, and a part of him prayed she didn't lose her baby because if she did, there would definitely be hell to pay. The type of hell fire that nobody would be prepared for.

"Alexxus!" Wild Bill yelled, making Lexxy's mind turn away from the thoughts of how the blood starting seeping from in between her legs, how she screamed out in pain and cried for Cocaine, and eventually, she passed out. When she woke up, her father was there, saving her.

"Sorry! No, not Baptist. This was all Carley; and I know that bitch ain't missin' no shifts. We would just be playing back into her hand. Take us to Vandy."

Lexxy realized something; she hadn't seen or heard Cocaine's voice this entire time, something was wrong. First, she looked in the empty seats and realized he wasn't in there, and then she looked into the trunk, and there was her man with his hand still covering his rib, with his eyes closed.

Blood seeped through the holes of his fingers, and

she wasn't sure if he'd be able to hold on much longer. With his breathing shallow, all Lexxy could do was hope for the best and pray for her man. She loved Cocaine more than she loved herself. She knew as a doctor what needed to be done, but she wasn't in any position to be trying to help him, nor did she have anything in the truck with them that would be of any use. All she had was the power of her tongue to pray and her hands to help hold the blood in.

She pressed her hands against his side and said a quick prayer, asking for this not to turn out the way it seemed to be headed.

Lexxy looked around the car as her mind finally started to catch up. The answers she didn't think she needed at first were now pinging off the walls of her brain, and she had to know what was really going on.

"So…I guess you're not really dead?" Lexxy laughed, trying to cut the tension in the car. She realized all they'd been through, but someone had to say something, to do something.

Juaqeen turned around and looked at Jayla who was rocking herself, sitting next to Wild Bill, then back at Lexxy. He could see what his son saw in Lexxy. She had rich chocolate skin like they did, and she was just pretty and good to look at.

"Didn't you know? It's hard to kill a Blackwood. Coco'll be fine. This is, well, I guess your grandfather-in-law, Roman."

He flipped the visor mirror down to see Lexxy better. "Hello, pretty girl."

Lexxy couldn't believe this. Three generations of the

Blackwood men were in the same car at the same time, and it wasn't in a dream.

"And this? Has she said who she is?" Lexxy asked, hoping someone knew who the mysterious female prisoner was.

"That used to be Jayla, Cocaine's mother. We're going to get her back to where she used to be. That's on my life."

Lexxy wished she could see the woman's face. Cocaine had only showed Lexxy two or three pictures of his mother, since Ella Mae only had a few. Lexxy had also been able to read the letters Cocaine's mother had written him, and she wondered how such a beautiful person, or what seemed to be found herself in this position.

Lexxy's face held a shocked look, and Juaqeen tried to stifle a laugh. Everyone in the car looked somewhat shell shocked.

"Once everyone is better, healed and sealed, I'm sure we're all going to have to have a very, very long discussion. This mixed family has been through a lot from what I understand. You're Dutch's daughter, but not his daughter because Wild Bill is your father. Finding out that little secret couldn't have been easy, but you seem to have adjusted well to the situation."

Lexxy thought about it, and he was right. She had adjusted pretty well. She didn't let it upset her too much. Besides, Dutch had been tripping, and he made it much easier to let go of him by the way he was acting. If he would've been acting like he had some sense, it possibly would've made it harder for Lexxy to accept the truth, but you couldn't be acting like a cry baby thinking shit was going to work out in your favor.

The hospital came into eyeview, and Lexxy wasn't sure who she should be more worried about—herself, Cocaine, or Jayla, her mother-in-law, even the thought of that fucked Lexxy up.

She wondered about her own mother and how she must've taken the news of her missing. Junie was a strong woman, but everyone has a breaking point, and they'd all reached theirs.

Jayla, who was almost void of mind, looked out the window, wondering what was to come. Though she could remember what happened to her, everything seemed like a nightmare, like a terrible dream. She was happy to have finally been rescued, but just how far would she be able to go or make it? Things were different. She'd only been able to go outside once a month, so the outside world was very strange to her. She'd been living in a cage, trapped by her own children, who she knew didn't know who she was, but just the fact that they could do this to a woman messed her up. What type of monsters had she given birth to?

R oman pulled up to the front of the hospital and dropped everyone off. Cocaine wasn't even awake when they'd pulled up. Wild Bill ran into the hospital, trying to explain to the nurses that they needed help.

When the doors and the trunk to the SUV opened, the nurses seemed as if they were thinking the same thing —these people seemed like Superheroes that couldn't be put down. The nurses got each of them on gurneys, seeing as how none of them could walk, and Cocaine was barely breathing. The bullet had affected his breathing, being that it was stuck in between his rib cage.

The nurses worked quickly and effectively, tending to each one of their cases.

"We'll let you know something as soon as we do," one of the nurses said as he went to the back with the rest of them, following closely behind the patients.

Roman, Juaqeen, and Wild Bill sat in the waiting room. As fathers, they shared a common fear—losing their children. Though Roman had just now become a part of Cocaine's life, he'd always for the most part kept an eye on him and knew what he had going on in his life. He was even able to keep up with the fact that he'd come to Tennessee, but now that the cat was out of the bag, there was no point in him saying anything about what he knew. That would only piss Juaqeen off, and they had enough going on already.

Wild Bill feared having to call Junie and let her know what happened. He hoped that by the time she got to the hospital, they'd have some news about Lexxy and Cocaine. Wild Bill and Junie had grown extremely close, even closer than they used to be, and it hurt him to know that she was hurting. She'd been blowing up his phone, but he was honestly too afraid to answer, to have to give her bad news, but now, it was unavoidable. He knew if he actually called her, his voice would break, and he needed to prepare himself to be strong for her, so he sent her a text instead. She responded quickly, saying that she was on the way.

Denise and Ella Mae had been by Junie's side since Wild Bill told her that he was going to get Lexxy back, and they refused to leave. Since the wedding, Ella Mae stayed in Tennessee so she could be with her grandson and new granddaughter, and she had become very fond of Denise, Junie, and Wild Bill.

Cocaine promised he'd sell her house for her and that she could stay with him, but she wasn't sure if she was ready to let go of her house just yet. She loved her home; it was where Juaqeen was raised, where she fell in love with Roman every day, time after time, so letting go of her house wasn't something she figured she'd ever do. Ella Mae hoped to keep it in their family for as long as it would keep standing.

Wild Bill also neglected to tell Junie about Juaqeen and Roman. That wasn't something you said through text because no matter what, it just wasn't going to come out right. Plus, it would seem like some type of mental break, so he figured it would be best if they all just saw it for themselves.

About forty minutes later, Junie, and Denise flew into the hospital. Ella Mae decided that she would go and park the car, and she needed to be by herself for a little while. She'd been praying all night for Lexxy's safe return and hoped Cocaine wouldn't get hurt in the process, but a hospital visit could only mean a few things, and that was enough to ruin her.

Ella Mae was a strong prayer; she was from the old school, so she needed to go be by herself so she could get herself together, pray for everyone's nerves, and of course, give it all to God and ask that his will be done and be accepted. Ella Mae knew all too well that that wasn't an easy task, but you had no choice but to accept the Lord's hand that he deals.

Junie had on sweat pants and a t-shirt, unusual wear for herself, but she needed to be comfortable in case she had to get 'em up with somebody. It'd been a long time since she had to show out, but the world wasn't going to be able to get away with too much more, and this was the line, the last straw. Denise followed in with her.

Denise had never really had much of her own life, even when she tried or wanted to. How could she? She had to focus and worry about Lexxy all the time. She wasn't jealous; she just hoped at some point all of their lives would get themselves together so she could have a life of her own. Denise wanted to fall in love someday, maybe get married, and have a few kids of her own, but she didn't know how that would be possible if she couldn't ever stop worrying about her friend.

Junie ran up to Wild Bill, throwing her arms around him.

"What happened? Where is she?"

"She's in the back. We don't have any information yet, baby, we'll have to wait."

"And Cocaine? Is he alright? Are you alright?"

"Calm down, baby. I'm fine," Wild Bill said, rubbing Junie's face. She returned his affection by kissing his hands. Just feeling his touch was beginning to soothe her.

"But, I need to tell you something, and you definitely gotta sit down for this."

Junie's eyes lit up with alarm. She just knew this was bad news. She hoped it wasn't, but what else could it be?

Denise took a seat next to Junie, and for some reason, she also had a bad feeling, that the news Wild Bill was about to tell them was going to be life changing.

"So, you see those two men sitting over there?" Wild Bill pointed to Roman and Juaqeen who were sitting by the window. Junie hadn't even realized anyone else was in there with them. Her mind was in one place, and that was her children.

Junie looked over to the window, and she just knew she was seeing shit.

"That one man…he looks like—"

"That's because he is."

"He's who?" Denise asked. She had no clue what they were talking about.

"How is that even possible? Bill, what the fuck have you gotten yourself into in just a few hours?"

"Who is he?" Denise yelled, frustration seething through her teeth.

Junie turned to look Denise in the eyes and said, "That is Juaqeen Blackwood, Cocaine's father."

Denise burst into laughter, hysterical laughter at that. She didn't have time for the crazy shit they were kicking at her.

"Yeah right! Back from the dead, the great Juaqeen Blackwood."

Denise thought this was hilarious; she even slapped her knee and started slipping out of her chair.

Juaqeen saw Wild Bill was having a conversation with two women, one he remembered as Junie, so he decided to come over.

"Junie, how are you?"

Junie rose from her seat and touched his face, and then moved her fingers down his arms. She couldn't believe this was actually happening. The last time she'd actually laid eyes on Juaqeen, he was making plans with Dutch, and now, here he was, supposedly dead, but obviously not.

"Boy, y'all got some explaining to do, and tell the story really slow, since we're waiting to hear some news."

Denise was just as confused as she was before they said it. This made no sense. Juaqeen was supposed to be dead.

Juaqeen introduced his father to the ladies, and they all had a seat so that Juaqeen could explain everything that transpired over the last twenty or so years.

ocaine's eyes shot open, piercing with fire in them. The entire time he was out, he could still hear what was going on around him. He heard Lexxy's prayers, he heard his father's voice, and he remembered his mother, his mother saying that Paul and Quentin were his brothers. That just couldn't be real. She had to be mistaken, but at this point, none of that mattered.

Like a vampire, Cocaine felt a blood lust rushing through his veins. He needed to kill, and he had at least four targets that he was done playing with. He'd given everyone time to get themselves together, to turn away from their mistakes, but they didn't, and now, it was time for him to hand out some street justice. An eye for an eye type shit. Family or not, Cocaine didn't give a damn. He was going to end Paul's life for sure for shooting him, for being a punk ass nigga because his brother was getting his ass whooped. He was going to kill Quentin simply because his ass needed to be knocked back down to size. He needed to be brought down a few notches, and then of course the obvious, they took his wife. They ran her into an interstate wall and fucked her up, which in return had Cocaine fucked up.

Though he was lying in a hospital bed, he'd

completely forgotten all about the fact that he'd been shot in the rib. None of that even mattered at this point. He was attached to a heart monitor, had an IV in him, and even an oxygen mask.

"What the fuck is this?" he asked himself aloud.

Cocaine began ripping the oxygen mask off his face, removing the bandage that covered up his IV, and tried to get out of bed, but he was sorer than he thought. Cocaine was like Superman, nothing could really fuck him up, but that rib shot was his kryptonite. He tried getting out of bed again, but he couldn't move. He was too weak, and the pain was just too much, especially since they'd just given him another shot of Morphine, the pain meds hadn't kicked in yet, and he could feel everything.

Cocaine kept bouncing his back against the pillow, blaming himself for everything that happened. If he would've killed Dutch, none of this would have happened, or that's what he tried to tell himself. He needed someone else to blame other than the people who did this to his family. He even went as far back as to think about how this was partially his father's fault too. Had he not done business with Dutch in the first place, he would've never "died," and Cocaine would've been raised by his father, but then, he would've never met Lexxy, the woman he loved, who he wouldn't trade for all the world, not even a second a chance to grow up with his father.

Cocaine would've growled if he could have, but he was so angry and confused, he couldn't figure out what to say.

He closed his eyes and tried to envision Lexxy. Though he knew he wouldn't be able to see what was going on, that was better than what he had previously thought about. He wanted to picture her healthy and not in any direct danger, but with everything they had going on, there was no way of knowing for sure.

The door to his room flew open, and like the royalty he was, Juaqeen floated into Cocaine's room.

"Son, how are you feeling?" he asked.

"I don't care about me. Where's Lexxy? How's my wife, my baby?"

"We don't know yet. We're still waiting to hear. The doctor said you're as healthy as a horse, so you'll be fine, but if I know you like I know myself, and I'm sure we're the same, you gotta think rationally. This has been a strain and taken a toll on this entire family. Don't do nothin' to add more stress."

Cocaine couldn't believe his father was talking to him like this.

"No offense, Pops, but I'm not a little boy anymore. You can't tell me what to do or how to feel. Shit, I'm about to rid this family of the problem just as soon as I get up out of here."

Juaqeen nodded his head and stroked his goatee. "Let me tell you somethin', ain't nothin' wrong with gettin' revenge, I know it all too well. That taste of blood you got boiling inside of you ready to spill over like a fuckin' volcano. I know it. It's all ready to erupt in the worst way, but let me tell you somethin', you're a man, and a man's first priority should always be his family. You have a family that needs you now more than they ever have.

Take care of them first, and then, I promise you, I will help you do whatever it is that you want to do. My word is my bond."

Juaqeen placed one of his hands on the back of Cocaine's shoulder, and then the other in his hand, reassuring him that he had his back, period.

Juaqeen's love and value of family was something Cocaine knew was important, and he would stand in agreement with his father. It was a necessary evil for now, and he would be there for his wife and the rest of his family in this trying time.

"Ok, Mrs. Blackwood, though the bruises to your face and the rest of your body need some time to heal, you'll be just fine. Unfortunately, you did miscarry. I'm so sorry for your loss. Your husband is just a few rooms down, and he's requesting to see you. While you need your rest, if you're feeling up to it, you can see him when you're ready," the doctor who was overseeing Lexxy's diagnosis said, and he walked out of the room.

Lexxy knew this was a possibility. She knew in her soul that she lost her baby. She knew she'd never get to see what could've been of her baby. Carley had taken that away from her.

The pain of the day had finally settled in. She was happy that Cocaine was ok, but was she? She didn't know if she'd ever get over something like this. She'd seen this scenario a thousand times over in the hospital; she was a doctor after all. She'd watched and read case studies about blunt force trauma to the uterus, making it impossible for a baby to survive, but she never knew this would happen to her.

The pain she felt in her stomach was nothing compared to the pain she felt in her heart. Her heart ached for the child she lost, for feeling guilty about it, and because she would have to reveal this terrible truth to Cocaine.

Lexxy's heart roared and rumbled, causing a loud, shrill scream to come out of her, over and over. She began punching at the air as if someone was in her face, preferably Carley. Tears overflowed, cascading down her cheeks like a broken dam that was unrepairable.

What was she supposed to do now? She hadn't been married for long, she hadn't been pregnant for long, and she hadn't even been well for that, and now, she felt like she was back to square one—lonely, and not pregnant. How was she going to tell Cocaine that she lost their baby? A baby that he was so happy to have. She tried not to think about it; she forced herself to try and believe Cocaine wouldn't blame her, because he wouldn't. He wasn't that type of person, but in the heat of the moment, guilt and shame overcame her, and she didn't know if she'd ever heal from this tumultuous moment.

After an hour of sitting and praying in the car, Ella Mae finally surfaced in the hospital. She had her purse, and inside of it was the "piece" that would restore balance to her family if the peace of the Lord didn't.

She believed in God and had an amazing relationship with him, but she also knew the Lord moved slowly sometimes because he worked on HIS time, and not their time.

Plus, Ella Mae knew how this went. She was the wife

of a drug lord, and she'd seen her fair share of mess. She knew how these battles could go. It was nothing for the enemy to show up at the hospital to finish the job, and she was ready for anything that may come. Though Ella Mae played the sweet grandmother role, because she was sweet, she was also crazy, and wasn't gon' keep on playing these games when it came to her family. She'd been alone for so long and didn't have anyone to worry about, but now, she did. She'd spent a lot of time away from Cocaine. She wasn't sure if she should ever reach out to him, and when he did, it changed her life. It opened her back up to a world she thought was gone long ago, but it wasn't.

She'd texted Junie before she came in the hospital to find out where she was, and it hadn't even dawned on anyone that Ella Mae and Roman were together before, that they were technically still married, so no one even thought to warn her about what was going on. Even more so, everyone was just so consumed with what was going on with Cocaine and Lexxy, nobody could even think about that.

Ella Mae strolled through the hospital, meeting Junie and Wild Bill.

"What are they saying? How are they?"

Ella Mae had prayed that the Lord wouldn't take either one of them and that they'd be ok, but she also knew the lord's will wasn't always what everyone wanted.

"Well, Cocaine was shot in the rib, but they were able to remove the bullet and take the pressure off the airway, so he'll be fine. He'll be just fine, and Lexxy…."

Junie's words trailed off. She couldn't even finish her

sentence. She wasn't ready to say it out loud. That was another reason why she hadn't gone in to even see her. She didn't know what to say. There was nothing she could say to make her baby girl feel better, so she figured she shouldn't say anything at all.

"Oh, baby, I'm so, so sorry." Ella Mae pulled Junie in for a tight embrace while releasing one of her hands to touch Wild Bill's face. Junie was so thankful to have Ella Mae in her life. She was like the mother she wished she had. She was understanding, caring, and emotionally available, nothing like how her own mother was.

"Where's Coco?" Ella Mae asked. She was eager to see her grandson, and she needed to see with her own eyes to make sure he was ok.

"Come on, he's right through this door. But, Ella Mae—" Junie began her sentence, but Wild Bill stopped her and shook his head no. He already knew Junie was about to tell Ella Mae who was waiting for her behind that door, but they hadn't told Juaqeen and Roman about her, so there was no point in telling her about them. Besides that, saying it was nothing like seeing it. Everyone could use a little good luck for the day, a little good will, and seeing them would make Ella Mae more than happy. It would be the reunion of a lifetime.

Ella Mae figured Roman wasn't dead. She received a check every month with his name on it—something she'd been getting since Roman disappeared. She tried to find him. She used the money he sent her to look for him for years, but even with an account and routing number, she could never find him. His money was practically untraceable, but she knew he didn't want to be found, and after six years of searching and coming up empty, she gave up hope that she'd be reunited with her husband.

Ella Mae knocked on the door three times and she opened it, alerting the people inside that she was coming in. When she stepped into the room, it took everything inside of her not to pass out, not to fall over.

Roman and Juaqeen turned around, smiling, just as surprised as she was. No one had told them that this was a thing, that she was even in Cocaine's life.

"Mama?" Juaqeen said as he went over to her before she almost hit the ground. Her knees were buckling underneath her, and she didn't know if she'd be able to stand up on her own two feet. Her son was supposed to be dead a long time ago, something she'd never truly gotten over, something she never completely came to terms with because of his sudden death. On top of that, the funeral held in his honor, just didn't seem personal enough. She'd made it all the way to the funeral celebration and never went inside. She just couldn't do it.

"Qeen, baby, is that you?"

Her glasses that were hanging around her neck were now around her eyes. She just knew her eyes were playing tricks on her. They had to be deceiving her.

"Yeah, Mama, it's me." Juaqeen hugged his mother, taking in her appearance. Though she was much older, she still looked the same, smelled the same, and her hugs were just as warming as they'd ever been. He didn't even realize how much he missed her until now. He always wondered how she was, but after being gone for so long, he figured it would be best to stay way. His father had managed to do the same, and he tried to follow his father's lead. Beyond that, they had been fighting in the streets of Haiti, so it wasn't safe for them to be in touch with any family members, ever.

"I guess I'm invisible," Roman said as he smoothed out his clothes, running his hands over his crispy black slacks. He looked down at himself, hoping he looked presentable. A check every month was nothing compared to actually seeing him up close, but Ella Mae wasn't even sure how she felt about this. On one hand, she was ecstatic to see him, her heart yearned for him over the years, as did her body, but she was hurt and upset. He'd left her one night, just completely left, and she'd never truly gotten over it.

Ella Mae released Juaqeen and walked up to Roman, sizing him up. She noticed how he'd aged, the way she had, but he still looked like the same old Roman to her with a few more wrinkles than before.

"Do I get a hug too?" Roman smiled and held his arms out.

Ella Mae turned her head to the side, and then she raised her hand and brought it down across his face, hard and fast like a lightning bolt striking the ground.

The spit flew from Roman's mouth as his head turned.

"I deserve dat," Roman admitted. He understood completely where her hostility came from. He'd been gone entirely too long, but the longer he was gone, the more he got used to it, but that didn't mean that he didn't miss her. He just did what he thought was best. He wanted to keep her safe and disappearing allowed him to do so.

"You damn right you do, leavin' me by myself to raise Juaqeen, and then he died, but didn't die, and now, Cocaine. This is too much. The damn Blackwood boys are going to be the damn death of me yet! Now move so I can get over to my grandbaby, you old coot!"

Ella Mae scolded Roman. She wasn't mad at her son; she was happy to see him, but Roman? That was another story.

As Ella Mae visited with Cocaine, Roman flashed back to the day he left. He couldn't forget it even if he wanted to…

Ella Mae was at home one cold, Sunday afternoon waiting on Roman to return home. Juaqeen was eight-years-old, and he was a sweet boy. He loved to drink hot chocolate before he went to bed, and Ella Mae's homemade recipe made it that much better. He loved his mother's cooking, no matter what she made.

Ella Mae had just gone upstairs to get the empty cup that she knew for sure Juaqeen left by his bed, as he did every night.

Before retrieving the cup, Ella Mae leaned down and kissed him on the forehead, pulled the cover over him, and quietly left his room, closing the door behind her. Though they were rich and had plenty of money, Ella Mae didn't want a cook, housekeepers, and a whole bunch of people in her house. She was a wife and a mother first, and a drug lord's wife last. Keeping her family's normalcy was the most important thing to her, but the crime life often interrupted her day to day life, and tonight, was one of those nights.

Ella Mae washed the dishes and finished cleaning up the kitchen from the dinner she'd made that night. She assumed Roman would be home by now, but he wasn't, and though she tried her best not to worry, she couldn't help it. She knew Roman could handle himself, but anything could happen to him when he was out on those streets, and she worried every night that he may never come home.

Ella Mae waited up most of the night for him to return, and when he didn't, she became nervous. She had no idea where he was, and it wasn't like she could reach him—he didn't have a cell phone, so the only thing she could do was pray that he came home.

At the kitchen, she sat there all night, praying for his safe return, and by six a.m., when he didn't come back, she cursed at God. Was he safe? Where was he? Was he held up somewhere? Had he been out cheating on her? All of these thoughts rushed through her mind, and she didn't know what else to do, but she couldn't let her fear and mood effect Juaqeen, so she did the same thing she did every week day; she got her son ready for school.

She made him breakfast and made sure his clothes were in order. She made sure he brushed his teeth, had his backpack, and she kissed him before he left to get on the bus. This was her normal morning routine, but after Juaqeen left, what was she to do? Her thoughts were now back on Roman, who still hadn't made it home.

After about an hour after Juaqeen left, a knock came at the door. In fear of it being the police or someone coming to let her know that Roman was laid out somewhere dead, she quickly yanked the door open, unprepared for what might be on the other side. To her surprise, there was no one there. The only thing on the long, wide porch was an envelope that read Puddin' Pop.

Ella Mae looked around to see if she could spot the person who left it, but there was no one outside, or so she thought at the time.

When the door was closed, she opened the envelope and there was money falling out of it, along with a white piece of lined paper.

Slowly, she opened it up, and her heart began to tear at the seams. Puddin' Pop was the nickname he'd given her when they were still young and just dating, and the letter was addressed to her as such. Normally, it would've been sweet and made her feel good, but in this instance, she just knew it could only mean the worst.

As she read over the letter, that was just a few lines, she realized she may never see her husband again.

"Puddin' Pop, you're the love of my life, and my world. You've made me the happiest man alive, and I was no one, had no life, and didn't deserve to live until I met you. Remember that, forever. I love you."

Ella Mae had no idea what this letter meant, but she knew her husband was never coming home, or at least not any time soon. With all of the pain she was experiencing, Ella Mae dropped to the ground in seething pain. The love of her life was walking away from her, and she didn't know why.

From the outside of the house, Roman watched Ella Mae through the window. He wanted so badly to go in and just say never mind, but there were so many people after him because of the lick he'd recently hit that made them even richer than were before, so rich that he had the money to leave the country and start over, to still take care of his family at home, and do really whatever he wanted to do.

Roman didn't have the guts to say goodbye to her face to face. He couldn't stand to see her reaction. He knew she would beg him to stay, that she wouldn't let him go, and he could never say no to his Puddin' Pop.

Roman placed his hand on the window of their downstairs living room, aching to be with his family, but this was the only way to keep them safe, so he had to go.

In his absence, though Ella Mae never knew, Roman had eyes on her at all times. She was always cared for, and when she got older, she was still looked after, still cared for.

Roman walked up behind Ella Mae, wrapping his arms around Ella Mae's waist, taking in her apple scent. The love he had for her could never die and wouldn't.

"Come on, Puddin' Pop. Forgive me, baby. I did wat was best for da family. I wanted you and da boy to be safe."

Ella Mae leaned into his embrace, and she considered what he said. This was what she'd figured all along, but that didn't soften the blow or make it any easier.

She wanted to forgive him, to let it all go, but that was all easier said than done, and anybody with a heart knew that, but this was her husband, the only man she'd ever loved. She would never dare give herself to another man, not then, not now, not ever.

"Come on, Mama. Forgive this old man. I'm tired of seeing him beg," Juaqeen said, reminding his mother of the young boy he once was.

"Yeah, come on, Grandmama. You got this old nigga in here with tears in his eyes."

"Watch ya' mouth, boy!" Ella Mae yelled, making Cocaine recoil.

"Sorry," he said.

Ella Mae turned around and returned his affections with a kiss. She didn't think about what he'd been through, whether or not he was clean. None of that shit mattered. She was just happy to have her man back.

"The Blackwood men all under one roof again. Lawd….give me the strength."

They all laughed, and for a moment, just a brief second, they were normal…they were a family, and they were together.

No matter how badly Lexxy wanted to see Cocaine, now just wasn't the time. She couldn't remember a time where she'd ever cried this much, at least not since she was a baby. At this point, it hurt to even think. She'd asked her nurse to keep her family out of the room until she could get it together, but it had been three hours now, and they were becoming restless.

Though Cocaine couldn't walk around, he was in a wheelchair ready to see his woman. Junie told him the bad news about Lexxy losing the baby, and ever since, he'd been waiting, trying to give her space like Ella Mae said she'd probably want, and he wanted to give that to her, but this was ridiculous. She wasn't the only person struggling with this; so was he.

Yes, he was a man, and he was supposed to be the strong one, but at what point did he get to break down? When was he allowed to feel something other than strong? Him losing the baby was a huge blow. He thought for sure, before this, his life was back in order, that he was moving on, but then this shit happened to Lexxy, and their lives were turned upside down once more.

Cocaine said he didn't think it was a good idea for

them to all go in at once, but Junie figured she wouldn't kick them all out if they stood together as a united front. Lexxy would be able to leave in a few hours, and Cocaine didn't want to take her home without knowing how much she was loved and cared for.

Juaqeen pushed Cocaine down the hall to Lexxy's room. Alongside them were Wild Bill, Roman, Ella Mae, Junie, and Denise. Lexxy's door was shut, her blinds were drawn, and it seemed very uninviting from the outside, but that wasn't going to stop Cocaine from seeing his woman.

Cocaine wasn't the type to ask—he demanded whatever he wanted, and though he was sympathetic to what Lexxy was going through, the simple fact that he almost lost her as well was enough to make him go crazy. No, he didn't want to lose the baby, but losing the baby and then losing her would've been entirely too much.

Creepily, they all came into the room. Junie wished the sun was up so that she could get a little burst of sunshine in her room, but it was still dark outside, only adding to the negative feeling in the air.

"Hello, Sexy Lexxy," Cocaine whispered as he was wheeled up to her bed. Cocaine opened his hand, to take hers in his, but she snatched it away and turned her back to him.

She didn't want to see anyone, not even Cocaine.

"Baby, don't act like that," Junie said from the other side of the bed, and for the first time ever in her life, she rolled her eyes at her mother.

Junie couldn't believe what she was seeing. Her daughter was respectable and wasn't the type to act out, but she was, and this wasn't the time to bring it up. She knew she was suffering, and that alone was something she couldn't fix, nor could another person other than herself. Only Lexxy knew what she was feeling.

"Alexxus," Wild Bill called out to her as he walked up to the bed.

Even Wild Bill was ignored, something she never did. She loved her father and respected him on a level that most humans could never even imagine, but she wasn't in the mood to see or hear any of them. Being alone was something she desperately craved, and after telling the nurse that that was what she wanted, and they still popped in, they were disrespecting her wishes. Normally, she would just tell them how she felt, but at this moment, she was having a hard time vocalizing anything. She almost felt like a mute, it was almost impossible for her to say anything.

Even Denise, her best friend tried to make things better. She came up to her and wrapped her arms around her while lying her head on Lexxy's chest. Any other time, Lexxy would receive her best friend, love on her, and take in her kindness, but not right now. She didn't want to be touched or even seen. If she could ever disappear in her life, this would be the perfect time for her personally to do so.

"Lexxy, I'm so, so sorry. I'm so sorry." Denise apologized several times, trying to comfort Lexxy, but it had the opposite effect.

"Can y'all just leave? I don't feel like being bothered. I appreciate everyone coming to check on me, but I need to be alone."

After several attempts of trying to get Lexxy to be physically active with them, she decided to just say how she felt, regardless if they liked it or not.

"Well, sweetheart, we just wanted to check on you, and none of us think you should be alone."

Ella Mae voiced her opinion as she stepped up from the back. She didn't want Lexxy to be upset with them, but someone had to say it. Ella Mae was definitely worried Lexxy might try and kill herself if they weren't around. She had a dark cloud, an evil presence surrounding her, and Ella Mae didn't want her to let this feeling fester. She figured she wouldn't just be ready to get over it that easily, but she also thought Lexxy would want the family's support.

"No disrespect, Mrs. Ella Mae, but I'm not in the mood. Do you see my eyes? I've been crying my eyes out, and I want to be by my damn self. See, that's the problem —this family don't know how to respect privacy, and that was all I requested. I need time to regroup, to gather my thoughts!" Lexxy yelled, shocking the hell out of everyone.

"You ain't the only person in pain, Alexxus! Shit, what, you think I'm over here just lettin' that shit go? Nah, I'm hurt too, but I can't even be hurt with you because you don't wanna be bothered."

"Cocaine, shut up! This isn't about you! I'm sorry, for one minute, the spotlight isn't on you, and you don't know how to take it!"

Everyone in the room stared daggers at Lexxy, they couldn't believe she would even say anything like that, and Denise was surprised to have heard Cocaine call her Alexxus. He'd never called Lexxy by her real name.

Tempers flared, and everyone was in a state of disarray, but this wasn't the time nor the place to let their shit fly off the handle.

"You know what, why don't we just let her be, y'all. Lexxy, we gon' be right outside, baby, if you wanna talk or see one of us. Come on, let's clear out," Wild Bill instructed the family, and they all followed his lead by leaving the room.

It was sad to see Lexxy like this. Cocaine lingered for a few moments after everyone left out of the room because he wasn't done speaking his peace.

"Lexxy," Cocaine stuck his hand up on the bed to hold hers. "We're married, and even if we weren't married, I would say what I'm about to say to you. I love you, and I'ma be there for you, forever, but you gotta let me love you, let me be there for you. Don't push me away from you. You're my queen, with or without a baby, but if you push me away, I'll have lost two people that I care about. I can't lose you too, baby."

Cocaine planted a soft kiss on her hand, and then he rolled himself out of the room. Lexxy wished she could turn her emotions back to the happy switch, but that wasn't happening today, not anytime soon anyway.

The only thing Lexxy could do was sleep. That was the only place her mind was truly at rest, or at least it had been, but not this time.

Lexxy drifted off to sleep, and as soon as her dream appeared, Carley's face came into view. Lexxy had never imagined herself to be much of a killer, but you know what Tupac said, "I ain't a killa but don't push me."

Lexxy had been pushed farther than ever before. She'd been robbed of an opportunity to be a mother, and Carley would suffer the way she had, at the hands of Lexxy.

Carley might have thought Cocaine and the other men were coming for her, but she would be wrong. Lexxy was not about to play, and bossing up wasn't even the proper term for what she was about to do. It was time for Lexxy to release the beast that really lived inside of her, and as soon as she was able to, Carley's ass would be grass.

"Junie, Bill, how are you? I came down as soon as I heard Lexxy was here. How is Cocaine?" Doctor Graham, their favorite doctor came out asking.

"He's ok. He's visiting with Lexxy still. Doctor Graham, what are you doing here?"

"I occasionally float, sometimes when other hospitals are short staffed, Junie. What's going on? What happened?"

Junie looked at Wild Bill and then at Ella Mae, and of course to Juaqeen and Roman. What could she say that would make enough sense or that wouldn't condemn them all? They lived very crazy lives, so it wasn't much that she could say, so she decided to help try and distract him with another question.

"Doctor Graham, let me ask you a question, is there anything you can tell us about another family member who came in with us tonight; her name is Jayla Blackwood."

Doctor Graham's eyes shot open wide. He had heard about this woman but didn't even think about her possibly being related to Cocaine and Lexxy, though Blackwood wasn't a common last name. From what he knew, Jayla had endured a lot of physical and mental trauma. Most of her wounds and bruises were old, some that never properly healed, so her skin was discolored in certain areas. Her hair was matted to her head, but also bald in some places. She stunk like she hadn't had a bath in quite some time. Doctor Graham wasn't over the case, this was just what he'd heard.

"She's family? What relation? I hate to ask, but I don't want to break the confidentiality of the patient."

Juaqeen overheard what Doctor Graham was saying, and he approached them.

"Hello, I'm Juaqeen Blackwood, Cocaine's father, Jayla's husband. Do you have any information on how she's doing?"

Doctor Graham couldn't be sure, but he could have sworn he'd heard Cocaine talking about how his mother and father were dead; this was all very confusing, but now, Doctor Graham could see possibly what was going on with Jayla. Wherever she had been, it was a dark and either cold or stuffy place. Jayla was having a hard time breathing, so the doctors put her on oxygen and began running a series of tests.

Because Doctor Graham was a friend of the family, since he'd been the one to save Lexxy's life, Junie felt confident that if need be, she could ask him to look after her.

"Hello, it's nice to meet you. What a large family you're turning out to have, Junie. So far, all I know is that they're running several tests, and for now, they're just trying to get her cleaned up and possibly talking so the doctors can figure out the best treatment plan based on the cause of her injuries."

Junie turned to face Juaqeen with pleading eyes. She knew how this sort of thing normally went—you didn't say a word, but if saying something would help save Jayla, then he would have to spill the beans.

Junie and Juaqeen went back and forth explaining the entire story the best way they could. The three of them were ducked off in a corner, having what seemed like a very sad story to the people walking past them, and though it was sad, it had sort of a victorious vibe to it. The Blackwood family had been broken up time and time again, but they were reunited under the most unlikely circumstances.

"My, my, my. Well, that is quite the story, definitely book worthy. I can try to see if the doctor won't mind bringing me on, but there will be only so much I can do if he doesn't. Doctor Ruiz is a stickler and has a wooden log stuck up his ass. I'll do what I can, Junie. I promise, and when Lexxy's ready to hear it, let her know how sorry I am, and not to give up on living. She has so much life ahead of her, and I want to be there when she goes back to work at Baptist. She's a remarkable woman."

Truth be told, Doctor Graham had a little crush on Lexxy, and he felt bad for her for being in a family and even a relationship that seemed to keep her in danger. If he only had the side nigga gene and balls, he would've shot his shot, and it was for this reason, him liking Lexxy, that he would do whatever he could to help her family now.

Doctor Graham said his goodbyes and went straight upstairs to check on Jayla. If all of what the family told him was true, Jayla was going to need more than physical help. In his opinion, they might as well open up the looney bin and give her a padded cell.

The nurses around Jayla were moving back and forth, constantly asking her how she was, taking her blood pressure, checking on her, and all she wanted to do was get out of there. A hospital was just another form of a cage, even if they were trying to help. The hospital wasn't a comfortable place, and nurses made Jayla nervous.

Jayla looked around at the IV she was hooked up to, the many tubes coming out of her, and the nurses. One of them, Nurse Penny, reminded her so much of a friend from the past, Shannon. Shannon haunted her memory every day and being here only made it worse.

Jayla had been unconscious for several days now—the doctor at the hospital said that she would and that it was normal, but to keep an eye on her in case something changed. When Amir brought Jayla back to his home in Tennessee, he hired several nurses who were trained in the art of discretion, so Amir didn't have to worry about his secret getting out.

For the first few days that Jayla was out, he was angry, but not because she was asleep; he was angry because he couldn't figure out what Juaqeen was doing with such a beautiful woman. How did he manage to have someone like her? His only answer was money, and he had plenty of that.

Seven days later, Jayla woke up, confused, hungry, and of course, very afraid. She cried constantly, begging for Cocaine, and no one would allow her to see him, at least that was how she took it. She didn't even realize she was a real prisoner.

At first, she was hysterical. She lie in her bed, in her room that Amir had specifically set up for her, crying day in and day out. Sometimes, she wouldn't eat, sometimes, she wouldn't sleep, she might go a day or two without a bath, anything to be rebellious to Amir. She felt like as long as she was being rebellious, she was being loyal to Juaqeen.

It was rare that she'd ever see Amir, but when she did, he wouldn't speak to her, knowing that it drove her crazy, but once Jayla realized the game Amir was playing, the intimidation game, she started to play along, but that only lasted so long before Amir finally said what he wanted from Jayla.

One morning, while she was eating her breakfast, it had been about thirty days at this point, Amir came into the room. The nurses who were on staff at all times, as they were also maids, scrambled around the room setting another place setting at the table for Amir. Jayla didn't care if she was done eating or not; she wasn't going to dare sit here with him at the same table.

She threw her napkin from her lap to the table and began walking away, until Amir got in front of her, blocking her way from the stairs. She tried moving to the left, and then to the right, but she couldn't get away from him.

"Mmm…you're in a hurry I see…"

"In a hurry to get away from you. You've got me trapped in here like I'm Belle and you're the beast."

Amir ran his fingers alongside Jayla's arm, tickling her, but not in a good way. She wanted to vomit from his touch.

"I don't have to be a beast, and you don't have to be kept here like this. All you have to do is get Juaqeen to agree to do business with me, and you can go home."

There was no way in hell Jayla was going to do that. Amir was dangerous, and she couldn't trust him. This was the same man who'd stolen her right after giving birth, and if he was busy occupied with her, he'd leave her baby and her man alone. Besides that, she remembered the conversation she'd had with Juaqeen before Amir even came over; he told her he didn't trust him, and if Juaqeen didn't, then she wouldn't, and she wasn't going to no matter what.

"I guess I'll be here forever. I'll never help you, never."

Jayla crossed her arms as she stood her ground. Most of the people who lived in that house were servants and afraid of Amir, but Jayla wasn't. She found strength in knowing that she had the power to control him when it came to the safety of her family, even if that meant that she wasn't going to be safe. None of that even mattered.

In the days to come, Amir acted strangely; he would give Jayla presents, comment on her body, her hair, and her smile, and then he would end the day by asking her to do the same thing over and over again.

This went on for a solid year, but eventually, Amir became upset. He was a sick, twisted individual. He believed that Jayla was playing hard to get, that somehow, her silence and evil slurs were indicative of her wanting him, when it was the exact opposite. She hated Amir for keeping her away from Cocaine and Juaqeen. She'd thought about escaping many times, but she wasn't really crazy enough to try Amir's patience. She knew what he could take, and what he wouldn't tolerate, so she played it cool, but her answer always remained the same.

After a year of saying she would keep her mouth quiet, she'd come to terms with the fact that she may never see them again, and that was ok with her. For the most part, she was living comfortably. She had her own room, food to eat whenever she wanted, as many books as she requested, clothes…the list was endless, and Amir knew that. He knew she was too comfortable, so he planned to shake things up.

Jayla was in her room, preparing for bed, when the door flew open. She was butt naked in front of the mirror, trying to cover herself or hide.

"Amir, get out of here, now!"

Jayla tried to keep her naked body hidden, but all she had in the near vicinity were the clothes she was going to put on, and she was too afraid to move because of the look Amir had in his eyes.

He looked deranged, disoriented, like something jumped inside of his body and turned him into a demon.

"No, no, I don't think I will. You've been playing coy with me for a year now, and I'm tired of playing with you. You don't have to pretend like you don't want me; I know you do, and I want you too," Amir said as he began walking around the room, trying to get to Jayla, who was moving around the room, trying to stay as far away from him as she possibly could.

"Amir, I don't want you, not even in the slightest. I'm in love with Juaqeen; he's the only man I've ever wanted, ever, and that is still true. I don't know where you got this sick ass idea from, but you must have lost your mind."

Jayla backed up into a wall, and she was cornered. She tried to move around, bounce around even to any other side of the room that Amir wasn't on, but to no avail, she couldn't get away from him.

Amir tightly grabbed Jayla's arm, wrapping his fingers around her. Jayla wouldn't give him the satisfaction of seeing her cry. If she was going to get raped, that was bad enough, but she wouldn't let him know that she was in distress. She instead took a deep breath and thought about Juaqeen and how she would do anything for him and how she was about to.

Amir threw Jayla on the bed, and she put her legs up to try and protect herself, but Amir was much larger and stronger than she was. Though she got in a few kicks, he still had her pinned down to the bed, shifting his weight in between her legs to pry them open.

Amir put all of his body down on top of Jayla, and he began kissing her, almost sensually.

"You may have been Juaqeen's, but you're mine now."

Those words would forever haunt Jayla. Every time she closed her eyes, she could hear him saying those words.

If raping her wasn't bad enough, and it did get worse, he beat her. Sometimes every day, sometimes while he was raping her. If she didn't do what he wanted her to do, like being around when he came home, or if she didn't fuck him when he told her to, he'd beat her. Really, any time she started getting strong again, he'd beat her.

Jayla endured four years of this, and each time he'd beat her, it got worse and worse, but Shannon, one of the nurses, took pity on Jayla and tried to help her as much as she could.

Four years later, Jayla found out she was pregnant with Paul. She hated herself, and most of all, she hated Amir. She begged Shannon to give her something to kill the baby, because if she ever found her way back to Juaqeen, she felt like he wouldn't want her anymore because of a bastard child, but Shannon couldn't do it. She vowed to save life, not take it, so she couldn't provide the relief she sought. That just wasn't going to happen.

When Amir found out that Jayla was pregnant with Paul, he

hatched a new plan. He was going to use the child as a bargaining chip to unite the families, and to him, it was a fail proof plan, until Jayla had Quentin, and she was completely detached from the baby. Whenever she'd see him, she'd throw up, literally.

Years passed by, and she would never see the children, didn't want anything to do with them, and Amir had gotten tired of it. Though his sexual appetite had grown, it had gone away for Jayla because she wouldn't accept his children, and if she wouldn't accept them, he couldn't use them as pawns, so he locked Jayla down in the basement and kept her there, for years. Even years after they moved away from the house, he kept her down there, and as the years went on, she just wanted to die.

But twenty years in one place gives you a lot of time to think, and Shannon, good ole Shannon had always been by her side, until she tried to help Jayla kill herself. Though she said she wouldn't, she had to. She had to do something to get her out of this position, and going to the police was not an option, but Amir noticed the change in Shannon. She'd become more distant, wanting to spend more time with Jayla, helping her more, and Amir didn't like that. She was supposed to only be loyal to him, and she wasn't. Amir followed Shannon to the abandoned house one day, watching and waiting to see what happened, and he just knew something wasn't right. Shannon had brought more supplies with her on this day than she ever had before, and because of this, Amir knew her loyalties had switched, changed, and he had to do something. Before Shannon could even make it down the stairs into the basement, he put a bullet straight through her eyes, sending her flying down the stairs of the basement.

Amir's footsteps made Jayla shutter, and Shannon's dead body tumbling down the stairs made her scream and flip out.

"See what you did? This is your fault! This is all your fault, and now, because of this, I can't trust you, I can't trust anyone."

Jayla didn't know what to say, nor did she even have any words for him. Her heart was broken, and this was just the beginning of the terrible things Amir would do to her. Because of this incident, Amir locked her up in a cage, and only the henchmen were allowed to be around her, and they in true fashion of what Amir wanted, beat her, raped her, spit on her, and let her muster in her shit and pee for years to come.

After Amir passed away from a brutal heart attack and just old age, Paul and Quentin took over, and did as their father told them. They had no idea who this woman was, but it was undeniable to Jayla, these were her children. She didn't hate them; she wasn't even mad at them. She always hoped the day would come when she could tell them the truth about who she was, but until the day she was rescued, or died, she would have to keep that secret, and now, that she was safe, she was able to reveal the truth. She hoped now, she could start the healing of herself and her own family, but she didn't know how that would, or if it would ever be.

S everal hours later, the sun had come up, and it was a new day. Juaqeen was finally allowed to see his beloved Jayla thanks to Doctor Graham who if it was left up to Juaqeen, he would personally be hiring to bring in as a private doctor for any more mishaps they might possibly have, but Juaqeen, and hell, the whole damn family prayed that it wouldn't come to that.

"I'll go with you if you need, Juaqeen." Junie offered a helping hand. She couldn't imagine what Jayla was going through or had been through, but she figured maybe a feminine touch might help some.

"No, that's ok. I think I need to do this alone. After all these years, there's a lot we need to talk about, and I prefer to do it alone, but I'm thankful."

It was true; Juaqeen was very happy to have some family support, but he had no idea what Jayla was going to say when he went into that room, or if she would say anything at all, and he wanted to let her know that above all, he was there for her, the way he wished he would have been all those years ago. If he would've known, he would've saved her, he would've helped somehow. Juaqeen loved Jayla, and the fact that she'd been hurt, time and time again, and he couldn't save her, made him furious. The man who was supposed to be invincible, something like a hood superhero, a legend, couldn't protect the ones he loved. He'd failed her.

Juaqeen swallowed hard as he opened the door to Jayla's room. She was facing the window when he came in, letting the rays from the sun bathe her skin. It had been a long time since she'd been this close to the sun, where it wasn't shielded by a dark house and broken wood.

When she heard Juaqeen come in, she knew who it was. It was a smell that she could never forget, that could never be mistaken. When they were together, he would often try to sneak up on her, but she'd always say the same thing, that his cologne was too strong, and she knew when she was in the presence of the man she shared her soul with.

"I can still feel you, in my heart, moving about like water flows down a river. It's a feeling you never forget and could never mistake. I remember the day Amir told me you'd been killed. He said it of course to hurt me, but deep down, I knew that wasn't true. I always figured if you died, I would too because your heart is stuck to mine like a wing on a butterfly."

Jayla turned over to face Juaqeen, who had tears in his eyes. If he blinked, there would be nothing to stop them from falling. His head was down, looking at his own two feet. He couldn't stand to look her in the eyes for the fear of seeing the pain pour from her eyes, although he could feel it, even from across the room.

"Look at me, Juaqeen." Jayla spoke softly. Her voice almost floating over to him.

Juaqeen looked up, his heart wrenching and tensing up in his body.

"Jay…I just—I don't…"

"Don't say anything. You let me talk."

Jayla had been thinking of what she would say if this moment ever came. She thought she'd be more nervous because just hours before, she was shaking, frightened of everything moving in the world, but in this moment, she wanted nothing more than to be able to tell her story, to be seen, since she'd felt invisible and abused for so long.

Juaqeen pulled up a chair and sat it by her bed. He slid his hand across the bed to meet with hers, and with a slight bit of hesitance, she reached back. She wasn't used to being touched out of love and affection. The last time she had been given such love was the last time she saw Shannon alive.

"The day I gave birth to Cocaine, Amir took me. He made a deal with the doctor to put me to sleep long enough for me to make it back to Tennessee. He paid everyone in the delivery room. When I got to his house…" Jayla's voice began to break as she recalled the demons that were memories of the past.

"When I got to his house, at first, he was nice, not normal nice, but kidnapper nice. He wanted me to make you agree to saying you would do business with him. I told him no, for a year straight, I told him no. I wouldn't give you up, ever, and when he realized he couldn't break me that way, he began raping me, beating me, isolating me from the world. I gave birth to two of his children; for him, he wanted to unite our families. I was always just a bargaining chip, but even then, I wouldn't give you up. I loved you too much; I love you too much to do that to you."

Jayla took a break from speaking to look at Juaqeen and see what he was feeling. She could see guilt written all over his face and his body. She reached for his face, and he grabbed her hand and placed kisses on the inside of it, all the way up her wrist.

"Baby…I knew you were a rider, but damn. I wish you would've made the deal. Don't you know I'd rather have you than anything else? I would have much rather had you than the money and the clout. You're worth more than that."

"I was worth more than that, but now, now I'm this. A shell of what used to be a happy woman."

Jayla criticized herself with a harsh truth. She tried not to think about it. She didn't want to hurt herself any more than she already was, but she'd even stayed away from the mirror for the fear of what she might look like. In saying this, she turned her head away, now feeling like Juaqeen's eyes were all over her, scrutinizing the way she looked.

Juaqeen stood up and pulled her face back toward his, and he looked at her, really looked her. Her face was sunken in, permanently from where Amir had hit her in the face with a crowbar. She was able to have the bone in her face reset, but it never properly healed considering she endured many beatings from Amir.

Juaqeen sensed her skepticism; he knew what she was afraid of. One of the many things he'd always commented on was her beauty, but it wasn't just her outside beauty that he loved. Jayla was one of the smartest, kindest, strongest people he'd ever met. She'd put up with a lot from him—late nights, not coming home, different women making false accusations, business meetings, dead bodies. Through it all, Jayla stayed true.

"Don't turn away from me, Jay. You're still as beautiful to me today as you were then. I don't care about all that. When I see you, I don't see what happened to you, I see strength. I see that you loved your family so much, that you sacrificed yourself time and time again, but baby, that's over. That's done. Once a queen, always a queen, and you were Mrs. Blackwood all these years, with or without the paper that says so. We told them your name was Blackwood, you know, since you're supposed to be dead and shit. I don't want no raised questions, but I think we're good. The doctor who's been checkin' on you is cool with Coco's in-laws, so we're good."

Jayla already knew Cocaine was married. While she was locked in her cage, she could hear Lexxy shouting over and over again about how her husband was coming to save her. How he was going to fuck them up when he found her. At the time, she didn't realize she was talking about her son, not until she came out and saw what was going on and she was able to put two and two together.

Paul and Quentin were her children—children she never got too close to, children she couldn't see herself being the mother of, but she was, and even though she wasn't close to them, being that was one of the only choices she had, things were different now. She could be close to her children without there being some type of blow back, some type of consequence. She could have all of her boys together, happily, well, if they could get along.

Jayla and Juaqeen continued talking, telling each other everything they'd missed, and Juaqeen tried to fill in the holes that were created even within the last few days, like the fact that Carley was the one who helped take Lexxy, and she was Quentin and Paul's sister.

Jayla had never met her, and now, she hoped she never did. Jayla knew Lexxy had miscarried while they were in the basement. The scream she let out while it was happening, the way she cried. Lexxy sounded like a wounded animal, and Jayla of course wouldn't wish that pain on anyone, at least no one innocent.

"So, what do we do then? Three Blackwoods back from the past. How do we move forward? You've been in Haiti all this time with your father. Are you going to go back there?" Jayla asked, somewhat afraid of what the answer would be. She knew Juaqeen loved her, but she didn't know if Juaqeen would want to be with her, if he would stay with her.

"We do what we've always done, baby. We get you better, make sure our son is safe and happy, get back to being a family. You can finally get to have a relationship with your sons if you want; that's up to you, but I'm not going anywhere. I hated Haiti, and being up under Roman's ass all the time was driving me crazy. I would say we could go back to Texas, but there's so much bad blood there, so many problems. We might as well just stay here. Our son seems like he could use my help."

"I could use your help," Jayla said, almost shocked that it even came out of her mouth.

"Baby, I'll never leave you again, ever. You couldn't get away from me. Even if you wanted to, I wouldn't let you go, and this time, I'ma marry your ass before you get away from me."

The two of them laughed and laughed and continued catching up. Juaqeen didn't know what would happen from here on out, but whatever came their way, at least they'd have each other.

Though Jayla wasn't sure what her future held or how her sons, either of the three, would receive her, she had more to look forward to now than she had in a long time.

P aul and Quentin sat on their couch smoking a coke laced blunt, passing it back and forth.

"Ain't no way that woman was our mama. Dad said neither one of our mamas was shit, so he raised us. Ain't no way!" Paul shouted as he passed the blunt back to Quentin.

"I don't know, man. I don't know why that lady would say some shit like that if it wasn't true. We been lettin' our own mama get tortured down there in that basement for years. We never even thought to question Dad about it either. We just did what he told us to do. We a lot of things, but this, I don't even know what to call it," Quentin retorted.

Paul tried to think back to all the conversations he'd had with his father about their mothers, and not once had he ever mentioned either of them being alive. Amir always told them their mothers weren't fit to raise them, and instead of allowing them to struggle or stop their lives, he saved his children, making himself sound like a hero.

But the more he thought about it, there was one thing that stuck out to him. When Amir was on his death bed, he tried to speak to him, to say something to him that he thought maybe he'd made up or just heard wrong. His father murmured the word, *Jayla.* After he said that, Amir died, right there in front of him. It could have been the shock from his father dying that made him push that out of his mind until now, but either way, that didn't matter. They didn't know this woman from Adam's house cat. She was a stranger to them. The only mother they'd ever known was Carley's mother, and even then, they weren't that close with her because she was a bitch and was always begging for some shit.

"Shut up, Q. We ain't even got time to be thinkin' 'bout no shit like this. We gotta stick with the plan and move the fuck on."

"The plan? Nigga, that plan is dead! That woman is our mother, what the fuck is wrong with you!"

"I'll tell you what's wrong, but the problem isn't him, it's you," Dutch said as he came down the stairs, walking into the living room.

Quentin and Paul both turned around, staring in his direction.

"Me? Please tell me how it's me? The problem is yo' snake ass lurking around and shit. You lucky we even let you stay here, that we even fuckin' with you!"

"Letting me? Shit, I pretty much pay the bills around this bitch. Y'all treat me like I'm a coward ass nigga, when we all know that ain't the case. I left the wedding that day to regroup, to come up with a better plan. Considering y'all been keepin' this bitch that I thought was dead all this time alive in a fuckin' basement! If y'all didn't need the money so bad, you would've never reached out. Y'all have been havin' the bargaining chip of a lifetime in the basement the whole time and didn't know how to use it. I paid you for your silence, to keep that shit on the hush, and now, the bargaining chip is gone, so what am I paying for exactly?"

It was true. Dutch had gone to dig up Jayla's grave to use as a bargaining chip for his freedom of revenge from Cocaine against him. Dutch knew his reign was over, and he knew he didn't have the firepower to defeat Cocaine and the people who followed him. He was getting too old for this shit, and now, his chance was gone. He would for sure die now, and there was nothing he could do about it.

All the years he'd spent underhandedly ruining other people's lives, killing people, taking their money and legacies were now coming back to bite him in the ass. Karma was coming to beat his door the fuck down, and there would be no escaping this.

"You payin' for us not to kill you, nigga. Don't forget, you called us, begging us to take you in to keep you safe, and we been doin' that. Don't nobody even know where you at!" Paul continued yelling.

Luckily, they'd kept the fact that Juaqeen and Roman were there to help save her; they figured it would come in handy eventually.

Quentin was usually the one who would flip out over some shit like this, he was the uneasy one, but Paul was the calm one. Quentin was always flying off the handle, being irrational, but at this point, he didn't know who he was. He was raised by a monster, a man that taught him how to be that crazy, though it was already in his DNA.

Dutch needed the protection, Paul just wanted to kill Cocaine, and Quentin was confused. He didn't know what to do. He didn't want to betray his brother, to upset him, but he'd always wondered what his life would've been like with a mother. He wanted to know if the reason his mother left him was to be with another man, to have a better life, or if it was because of what Amir said; that she was truly just trash, and now, he could have those questions answered. He just needed to reach out to Cocaine without his brother or Dutch knowing.

Lexxy and Cocaine had long gone home, but Jayla had to stay for several days after the fact, and because of that, Juaqeen and Roman wouldn't leave her side. While the doctors ran their tests, they were amazed that a person, no, a woman, could endure the bruises and injuries that she had and still be alive.

Her body was broken down and rebuilt over time, but there were some scars she just couldn't get rid of even if she wanted to.

"You ready to go?" Juaqeen asked as he came into Jayla's room. Before he'd come to pick her up, Juaqeen went shopping for her. He'd spent the weekend getting things to make her feel comfortable and like a human being again. While she was in the hospital, Cocaine made up several rooms at home for his father, grandfather, and mother for just in case. Regardless, he wasn't letting his mother stay in a hotel, even if she protested. He wanted her to be comfortable and happy, and what better way to do that than to make her feel at home, because she truly was.

Juaqeen wasn't sure of the latest fashions, but when he went to the mall, he of course balled the fuck out. Jayla wasn't a young woman anymore, but he wasn't into that sort of thing anyway, so he went to the department stores, getting help from the older women who would know what was hot and trendy. When he was satisfied with his purchases, he brought them to Cocaine's house and placed them in her closet. He chose a yellow dress with a burnt orange cardigan to go on top, along with nude sandals that strapped up the leg; the woman at the store told him the gladiator look was in for all ages, and he trusted her expertise even if she was just trying to get a commission.

Jayla wasn't sure if she was ready to go live a normal life just because she wasn't sure if she knew how, or if everyone would accept her. Though she wanted to believe she would be accepted, she came with a lot of baggage that people may not have been willing to deal with.

"I'm about as ready as I'm going to be, I guess." Jayla smiled shyly as Juaqeen approached her. He looked over the dress she had on, and she was still just as beautiful as she was before. He grabbed her hand in his and held it for a moment.

"Whatever you're feeling, it's all good. Everybody is waiting for you to come home. It's going to take some time, but we gon' be good. You trust me?" Juaqeen asked as he squeezed her hand.

"With my life."

"That's my girl. Come on, let's get out of here."

Jayla checked out her surroundings, and though she wasn't sure how things would be from this moment forward, she knew it couldn't get any worse. If she had any chance or hope of getting better and her family accepting her, she had to first forgive herself. She'd always done what she had to do for Juaqeen and Cocaine. Even in her saddest moments, she held true and held on to wanting to be of use to her family, but a lot of guilt and rage came with that. The way Amir went out wasn't fair. Jayla had always hoped she'd be able to kill him somehow herself, but she wasn't able to, and that was something she'd carry around for the rest of her life.

Juaqeen led Jayla to the car, and they rode peacefully to Cocaine's house. From the street, Jayla could almost see the house. When they arrived, she could see it was huge, but she wasn't surprised. If anything, she was just proud of her son. She was proud for all he'd accomplished even without his parents in his life, or any family for that matter.

Pulling up into the long, circular driveway, Jayla laid eyes on her family, new and old included, standing outside waiting for her. Lexxy had suggested them playing it cool and letting her get acquainted with one another when she was ready, but Cocaine said it was better to just rip the band-aid straight off than let it fester for days on end.

Their relationships had a lot of repairing to do, and it needed to start today.

Juaqeen threw the car in park and looked over at Jayla. "If this is too much, I can just—"

"No, this is fine. It's a lot, but it's beautiful. Don't worry, I'll be fine."

Jayla was just talking. She didn't know if she would be fine or not, but she said she would. Hopefully if she said it, that would make it true.

Looking over her family's faces, she'd had the chance to meet everyone while she was in the hospital, and what a beautiful family it was to be a part of.

Jayla reached for the door handle, and Juaqeen grabbed her hand.

"Woah, wait a minute, baby. You already know you don't open your own door. You're a queen, let me treat you like one."

Jayla's insides jumped around. It had been too long since she'd been treated this way, but what else could she expect from him? He was the only gentleman she knew, and she hoped she'd be able to raise her own son this way, but she wasn't allotted that opportunity, but just from looking at him, and the way his wife clung to his side, she could tell that he obviously figured it out on his own.

Juaqeen got out of the car and walked around to the other side to open the door for Jayla. As soon as her feet hit the ground, it was like a sonic boom blasted through her body. She knew there was no turning back, there was nothing to go back to from this point forward.

Slowly, she stepped out of the car and rose to her feet. As she walked up to the stairs, one by one, each member of the family came down and gave Jayla a hug, welcoming her to the family. After everyone, there was Cocaine. He hugged his mother tighter than he'd ever hugged anyone, breathing in her entire being.

"Oh, Coco," Jayla said as she embraced her son, and tears flowed from both of their eyes.

"My baby. My beautiful baby boy, let me take a look at you."

He stepped back and looked at his mother. Jayla was amazed by how much he looked like Juaqeen. It was like she had nothing to do with it, though Cocaine resembled his mother in the smallest ways, he was truly Juaqeen's son.

"We gon' just stand out here all day and let y'all stare at each other, or we gon' go inside? We got food waiting and ready."

Wild Bill was hungry and had been told that they couldn't eat until Jayla got there, and he didn't want to eat, more so, Junie told him not to spoil his appetite by getting some other food instead of waiting for the guest of honor.

"Let's go, y'all before my daddy starts acting out. You know he can't live without alcohol, and he can't go longer than two hours without food."

Everyone laughed and went in the house to feed Wild Bill and continue welcoming Jayla home.

Though it wasn't a party, it was a celebration. The Blackwood Family was together, along with Lexxy's family, and they were all together enjoying one another. The only person who was missing was Denise. She had to still go to work and make a living for herself. She'd promised herself that within the next few months, she'd be working for herself, a true business owner. Her dreams were to own her own restaurant, which was why she stayed at the diner for so long so she could get experience before she opened her own. She'd been taking business classes at the local college for the last few months, and if everything went as planned, she'd be able to have her own money, her own business, and her own life.

Like Lexxy, her parents had money, but she hated them, her father especially, and she would never take his help, even if he did offer it. She was self-made, self-paid, and a boss bitch in her own right. Saving money was the goal, and even though she wanted to be there for Lexxy and her family reunion, she needed her coins more.

While everyone was laughing, drinking, and enjoying themselves, even Lexxy who had been down in the dumps, had a moment's reprieve from the heart ache she felt from losing her baby. Cocaine's phone began ringing with an Unknown caller as the Caller ID.

Cocaine stepped away for a moment and went over to the side so that no one could hear his conversation.

"Hello?" Cocaine answered, wondering who'd be calling him from an unknown number.

"Listen, I know I'm the last person you'd think to hear from…"

"You damn right. After what you did to my wife, you still gotta pay for that, nigga. You, Carley, and your brother."

"Our brother, you mean," Quentin said in a matter of fact tone. It was true, they were all family, in a very strange sense.

"Nah, you ain't no brother of mine, same mama or not."

"Say what you want, but the shit done hit the fan, and we all family, period. You may not believe me, but I wanna bury the hatchet. I went my whole life thinking my mama was a dirty bitch who didn't want me, you thought she was dead, meanwhile, she was under our noses the whole time. Paul don't want nothin' to do with

y'all, but I can't say the same for myself. Call it middle child syndrome, but I always knew I didn't belong, but I'm asking for the chance to get to meet my mother as my mother and be a part of her life, even if not a part of yours, and then I'll pay for the mistakes I've made, but I ain't leavin' up out of this world knowing I had a mother and didn't at least try to make amends on my part."

Cocaine clung to the phone, holding it tightly in his hand, almost crushing it. He couldn't believe Quentin would call his phone, but Cocaine was a real nigga, and he appreciated the gesture, even if he didn't know how to handle it, even if he didn't know what to say about it. Though he'd been denied the opportunity to know his mother before, he wouldn't take that away from Quentin, even if he wanted to. He wasn't a heartless person; that just wasn't him.

"Look, I'll see what I can do. You ain't the only one that got fences to mend. I got a whole family 'round here that needs to be repaired, I don't know how you fit into that, but we'll just have to see."

"I can take that."

"Nigga, you ain't got no choice."

Cocaine ended the call, and even though he didn't know it, he was already acting like a big brother. Cocaine always wanted siblings, and he hoped one day he'd have them, but he was robbed of that too, at least it seemed like he had been, until now.

"Baby, you ok?" Lexxy asked as she walked up to Cocaine, placing her hands on his shoulders.

He took a deep breath and turned around, faking the funk for his wife, who unbeknownst to him, had her own agenda.

"I'm good, baby. Everybody enjoyin' the food, themselves?"

"Of course they are. Daddy's drunk, well, my dad, your dad, Roman, Junie. Ella Mae and Jayla are sitting off to the side having a talk; I can only imagine what they're talking about."

"Shit, you and me both, but how are you, my queen? How are you feelin'?" Cocaine asked his lovely wife.

"I'm ok as much as I can be. As long as I keep moving, I feel ok. I can't feel it if I keep going."

Cocaine didn't want her to cope like this. The first thing he would do when he got a chance was get his baby some counseling. He'd be damned if she didn't get her chance at a happy life over some shit that Carley did to her, but he wouldn't mention that to her until she was ready.

Over the last few days, he'd seen a look in her eyes he'd never seen in her before. It was a look he recognized in himself, but never in his sweet Lexxy. She looked murderous, and though he hoped she wasn't plotting revenge, he could see that she was at least thinking about it. He knew the scent of vengeance better than he did anything else. He just hoped when the moment came, she'd ask for his help and not go at it alone.

Cocaine kissed Lexxy on the cheek, and he walked away from her, leaving her in her own thoughts.

Lexxy watched from behind the wall. Her family was

happy, smiling, and happy with one another, why couldn't she feel the same way? Why wasn't she happy? Those were the things she found herself asking whenever she looked in the mirror or when she was alone.

Carley had to pay, and over the last few days, that was all she thought about—her revenge. Though she didn't want to use Lucky as a pawn, he was her direct line, a direct route to Carley. She wondered if he had any idea of what happened, if he knew what Carley did to her. Lexxy knew that Lucky had nothing to do with it either way, but that didn't stop her from being mad at him for not doing something, and this was the only ways he could get retribution in her eyes, even if he didn't know that that was what he'd be doing.

Lexxy took out her phone and sent Lucky a series of text messages, asking to meet him, to see him, and like an idiot, he fell for it. He truly believed Lexxy missed him, and that she wanted to see him, when in all actuality, she just wanted to get him away from the house long enough to get to Carley.

"Meet me tomorrow, Centennial Park, twelve o'clock, cool?"

"Of course. I'll be there."

Lexxy had already checked to see if Carley at work; Lexxy was a doctor after all, she had access to everything, even if she wasn't able to go to work. When she saw that her name wasn't on the schedule, she wondered where she would be, so she asked Lucky, making it seem like it was in their best interest for them to be safe and away from Carley.

"Where will Carley be? I don't want her to know, you know she's a little crazy."

"I ain't worried about her, but she'll be at home since she's off work. Don't worry about her. I'll make sure she don't know shit."

Lexxy hoped for the sake of her plan that Carley wouldn't suspect anything. Carley was in for a rude awakening, and her life was on borrowed time.

The next day, everyone was tired from the day's events before. All the drinking and eating had rendered most of them useless for the day. Everyone except Cocaine and Lexxy was able to rest well. They both had a lot on their minds. Lexxy couldn't wait for this day. She was anxious because her vengeance was nigh, Cocaine couldn't sleep because he needed to have a talk with his mother and father. He needed to speak to each of them about the phone call he received. Though he wasn't used to having to discuss anything with other people before he made a decision, he still respected the hierarchy of family.

Lexxy pretended to be asleep. She didn't want Cocaine asking why she looked so tired, because she truly was. She'd been up all night figuring out what she would do to Carley when she got her hands on her.

Cocaine crept out of the room as to not "wake" Lexxy, and he went down the hall to his mother's room. He knocked on the door several times, and when she didn't answer, panic began to set in. He hoped she didn't run away. He couldn't imagine how she felt, but he wanted her there, along with everyone else.

He decided to go to his father's room, assuming he'd

be awake. When he was a young man Juaqeen always woke up before the sun came up, not on no 'the early bird gets the worm' type shit, but because he said the sunrise reminded him of Jayla.

Cocaine went to Juaqeen's door and knocked lightly, remembering there were other people in the house asleep.

When his father came to the door, he was already completely dressed, jewelry included.

"Good morning, son. What's goin' on?"

"I need to talk to you, but have you seen Mom? I just knocked on her door.."

"I'm right here, baby. You ok?" Jayla asked, sitting at the table that was near the window in Juaqeen's room.

Cocaine looked over to her and then at the bed, and his lips turned up into a smirk.

"What y'all been in here doin'?" he asked slyly, wondering if his parents got it on.

"Not that, boy, get in here and close the door before you wake everyone up with that loud ass facial expression."

Juaqeen laughed at Jayla's word play and moved out of the way for Cocaine to come in the room. Cocaine took another look at the bed, wondering what they'd done or were about to do when he knocked.

"So, you said you wanted to talk to us?" Jayla said as she cleaned off the table.

"Yeah, we all need to sit down. Dad, you sit on the bed, ain't no tellin' what y'all was in here doin'."

"And if we were? We grown, and don't owe yo' ass no explanation."

"Shit, that's true. If Lexxy was well down there, I'd be tearin' her ass up, but that's beside the point. Listen, Mom, your son, well, one of them, Quentin, reached out to me. I planned to kill that nigga, no joke, for what he did to my wife, and of course, you, but before I send his ass to hell, he wants to clear his conscience, to meet you as his mother and not as somebody he helped abuse for years. Now, that's up to you, but I thought you should at least know."

Jayla's face went from a smile to a frown almost immediately. She wanted to meet her sons, to be close to them, but she didn't expect it to happen so soon or like this.

"And Paul? What about him?" Jayla asked.

"I don't know. Quentin called, he was speaking for himself, so that's your call, but I wanted you to know."

Juaqeen sensed the hesitation in Jayla, and he got off the bed and went over to her side.

"I don't want you to make a decision based on how anyone else feels but you. You're the only one who matters in this situation. Don't worry about how it'll make the next muthafucka feel. Worry about yourself, and then you decide."

Jayla didn't know what she wanted to do. On one hand, she wanted to have a relationship with her son, and on the other, she had to worry about Cocaine and Lexxy. Lexxy was in the same situation she was, and Cocaine, well he was blood thirsty like his father had always been.

"You ain't gotta decide today. You can do what you want, Mom, and take your time. Regardless though, I'ma kill them both. I can't let them niggas walk around living life when they helped to take away one from me."

Juaqeen wanted to be proud of his son for having such a strong sense of family, but times had changed, and if he'd learned anything in the last few days, it was that time wasn't on their side anymore. That things were different, and family, of any kind, still meant something.

"Listen son, I know how you feel. Shit, I wanna kill them lil' bastards my damn self, but whether you want to believe it or not, they're your brothers, and family… especially to us, is part of the values we stand on. What type of man would you be if you killed them? Who would you be if you did something like that? One day, maybe not any time soon, you'd eventually be upset and guilt ridden. I think you'd be better off giving them a chance of some sort. Give them a chance, see if they can change, and if they can't, then and only then, can you give them niggas a bullet."

Cocaine had a lot to think about, including what his father said. He didn't believe in giving second chances where they weren't deserved, but that was the point his father was trying to make. He wanted him to give them a chance to try and do better. There was so much to do and so much to consider, but for now, Cocaine was just happy to be in this moment.

"Ok, look, enough of that heavy talk, let's go downstairs and get some breakfast. I can smell bacon, what about y'all?" Cocaine said, changing the subject.

It had been so long since Jayla smelled bacon, it was almost a foreign smell to her, but it was good to be in a house where she could get a warm meal. That morning, she'd taken a shower, a hot shower for the first time in what seemed like forever. She was warm, fed, happy, and loved.

Juaqeen, Cocaine, and Jayla walked out of the room together, headed downstairs where Roman was drinking a cup of coffee with Ella Mae, Junie, Wild Bill, and Lexxy, who had magically snuck downstairs.

"Good morning, I was wondering when you all would make it downstairs." Ella Mae held her cup in the air, inviting them to take part in their morning conversation.

"What y'all old folks down here talkin' 'bout?" Cocaine asked as he grabbed a piece of toast from the table.

"I know you better put that toast down and go wash your hands!" In true grandmother nature, Ella Mae wasn't 'bout to play with Cocaine.

"Yes ma'am!"

Cocaine wondered what his life would have been like had he had his grandparents in his life. From what he could tell, Roman was pretty chill, laid back, but crazy all the same. Ella Mae was old school—a real big mama of the family, and he could've used that growing up. Had he known her, he would've definitely been a granny's baby because he was becoming one as each day went by.

"Good morning, Mrs. Blackwood," Cocaine greeted Lexxy on his way to the bathroom. She just smiled as he walked by. Lexxy wasn't in the mood for pleasantries. She was out for blood, and she hoped the breakfast conversation would distract everyone from seeing through her.

"Y'all have a seat, I have an announcement to make."

Wild Bill appeared from the kitchen with plates of food that Junie had been up all morning cooking. She started with the pancakes, French toast, and sausage balls and then she moved on to the bacon and eggs.

Junie came in following behind him with napkins and silverware for everyone. The dining room table was wide enough for all of them, but the table seemed so formal, and everyone, excluding Juaqeen and Jayla still had on their pajamas.

Once the food was in front of them, Wild Bill began making his announcement.

"As you all know, Junie is the love of my life, and she always has been. When I went to prison, I lost her to Dutch, and I thought I'd never get her back. I honestly never tried because I respected her union, but when you love somebody, I mean really love somebody, that shit don't ever die. I waited twenty-six years to get you back, and it ain't no way I'ma ever let you go again, Junie. You're more than a good woman; you're an amazing woman, my woman, and I want you to be mine forever. Now, you can say no, but I'm just gon' keep asking you until you say yes. I don't wanna hear nothin' about your divorce not bein' final. That shit gon' get handled soon enough. So, what you say? Me and you make this thing official, real official?"

From his pocket, Wild Bill pulled out a ring the size of a ring pop. It was huge, and the diamond sparkled and lit up the entire room.

Junie had taken her ring off when she and Wild Bill

got back together. It was inappropriate for her to wear, so she didn't. This was something she honestly didn't see coming. She hadn't had a conversation with Wild Bill about them running off and getting married or being together, so this was crazy, but exciting. There was no one else in this world for her. Her marriage to Dutch, though it was real, and they had many happy years together, she was nowhere near as happy with him as she had been with Wild Bill in previous years, and now.

Lexxy's face held nothing but shock; she was just as surprised as everyone else. Though this proposal wasn't romantic, not even in the slightest, she knew her mother would rather have the real thing. She didn't care about a show, or even about a lot of people showing up to see something like this. Lexxy just wanted Junie to be happy above all, and if this would make her happy, then Lexxy was in full support.

Junie's hands had been over her mouth, flashbacks of the past rushing her like crashing waves. She remembered falling in love with Wild Bill, the day she found out she was pregnant with their child, and all the time they'd spent together over the years, and now.

Wild Bill was the man for her, and there was no way she was going to let him go this time. She'd let him go once thinking that was what was best for her family, but every day for the last few years, she regretted it, and would do anything to make up for the time they lost together.

Wild Bill wasn't on his knee, he wasn't even dressed properly. All he had was his love and a ring, and that was more than enough for Junie.

"Of course, baby. Of course."

Junie held her finger out to receive her ring, and it fit like a glove, like it was made just for her.

"I love you, Bill."

"I love you too, baby."

The two shared a passionate kiss, and like they were in a room full of strangers, the whole family clapped.

"Alright, alright! Y'all, chill out. Now that that's out of the way, let's eat. You know a nigga's hungry." Wild Bill laughed at himself. His second hour of no food was slowly approaching, and no one would like him if he was hangry.

Breakfast was finally over, and the time was getting close for Lexxy to go and meet Lucky, except she wasn't going to do that at all. She was instead going to ambush Carley at home. Poor Lucky really thought this was his moment to get his woman back, or at least see her, and he couldn't wait. Instead of dressing like he normally would or even in a relaxed outfit, he took a shower, sprayed on some cologne, and put on his new joggers with a button down. He was acting like they were going on a date, when that couldn't have been further from the truth.

Lexxy didn't say anything to anyone when she left the house, she just disappeared, hoping that no one would miss her, and since she'd been trying to get some alone time, she thought they'd just chalk it up to her finally taking time out for herself if they did notice she was gone.

Lexxy put on a hoodie and grabbed her gun. She'd been saving it for a special occasion such as this, even though she never really thought she was going to have to use it, at least not in this way. She knew eventually she'd have to protect her family, but this was so she could protect her sanity. She'd been letting people get over on her for too long, and losing her baby was the last straw.

Lucky left the house right on time; leaving with enough time with thirty minutes left to spare. He sent Lexxy a text letting her know he'd be at the park waiting for her, and she sent him a simple ok with a smiley face, pretending as though she was going to be there to meet him.

On the way over, Lexxy thought about all the ways something like this could go, but it didn't matter. In every scenario, she knew she would get the upper hand on Carley because she had something that Carley didn't—anger and rage. She was beyond pissed and ready to tear this bitch up.

When Lexxy arrived at Lucky's house, she didn't pull up in the driveway. She didn't want Carley to notice the car. Lexxy was driving one of the many cars Dutch had given her in the past, and she knew she wouldn't recognize it, and if Carley was smart, which she was, she wouldn't be opening the door for an unmarked car. Since it was early, it could be the mailman, or even a Jehovah's witness coming to spread the good word.

She had a word to spread alright, but it wasn't the

good word. It was the undeniable word of getting her ass whooped and killed.

Lexxy parked her car at the end of the road and walked the rest of the way. She felt bad for lying to Lucky, and she still cared for him and didn't really want him to have anything to do with this situation.

When Lexxy reached the door, she knocked on it, not hard, but just enough to be heard, and from the outside, she yelled, "UPS!" She knew that would make anyone come to the door. She stood to the side where Carley wouldn't be able to see her right away.

As soon as the door opened, Carley came face to face with Lexxy. She tried to shut the door on her, but Lexxy was strong. She was pumping with adrenaline, the same type of adrenaline that helped mothers save babies from crushed cars, the same adrenaline that flowed through the veins of firefighters.

Lexxy pushed the door open, forcing her way in, knocking Carley to the floor. Carley had on pajamas and her house shoes, the kind that she could easily slip on and off.

"Zeke, go to your room!" Carley yelled into the kitchen where her son was.

What was he doing there? It was a weekday, and Zeke should have been at school, but that made no never mind to Lexxy; she would take the little boy too.

"No, Zeke, you stay, or I'ma blow your mother's brains out and splatter them all over the floor."

Lexxy knew the layout of Lucky's house well, and there was nowhere in the house for Zeke to hide downstairs or really for Carley to go.

"Carley…you thought I was going to let you get away with killing my baby? There is no way in hell you could've thought that."

Lexxy specifically wore her Timberlands so she could stomp Carley's ass before carrying her out of the house. Lexxy lifted her leg and let a powerful blow down on her stomach.

"Aggh!" Carley screamed in agony.

"That doesn't feel good, does it? Having someone put pressure on your stomach? How do you think I felt? I had a complete human being inside of my stomach, you bitch!"

Lexxy lifted her leg and kicked her again, but this time, in the face.

Carley's arms rose from her stomach to her face as blood poured from her nose.

"Please, don't hurt my mom!" Zeke yelled.

Lexxy looked up at the little boy and felt no remorse for Carley or for him.

"Fuck that! Fuck your mom. Did she tell you what she did to me? I bet she didn't. She killed my baby. Maybe I should kill hers."

Zeke was frozen in fear as Lexxy came towards him, gun in the air.

"Lexxy, please, not my baby. I'm sorry."

Lexxy grabbed Zeke by his shoulders, pulling him closer to her. "Lexxy, please," Lexxy mocked Carley. "You evil bitch. If you want me to stop, get your stupid ass up. You're leaving this house with me."

Carley rolled over and saw Lexxy holding Zeke, the

gun pointed in his back. "I'll do whatever you want, just don't hurt Zeke."

"Then get up and stop talking about it, bitch!"

Lexxy's eyes looked like fire was burning inside of them. Her pupils were fully dilated, and she hated to admit it, but this power felt good. She finally understood how Wild Bill, Dutch, and even Cocaine felt when they were running around serving justice to muthafuckers.

Carley rose with her stomach shouting in pain. She hadn't felt this way even when she gave birth to Zeke. She needed something for the pain ASAP. Carley walked over to the door and put on her shoes.

"You ain't gon' need those where we're going, but I guess everyone deserves to die in the outfit of their choice."

Carley didn't believe Lexxy had it in her to kill her, but she knew for sure that she would hurt her a little, and she knew people died every day from being beat to death, so she would play this as carefully as she could if only to save her son's life.

Lexxy pushed them both out of the house with a gun to Zeke's back still. Carley kept turning around to check on Zeke, who was crying.

"You better walk, bitch, don't keep turning around looking back here. It ain't nothin' for you back here."

Carley did as she was told and kept walking with Lexxy giving her instructions on where she parked the car.

When they got in, she made Carley drive, and she moved the gun from Zeke's back to Carley's forehead.

"Don't do nothin' stupid, bitch, or we gon' all die in this car, you understand me?" Lexxy growled.

"I—I do. I understand."

Lexxy was going to have Carley drive to one of the houses that Dutch owned. At this point, she didn't care about getting caught, nor did she care if there was more blood on Dutch's hands. He would get what he had coming to him too because in retrospect, all of this was his fault. He was the cause of all of this, and eventually, he would pay.

I t was now forty minutes after the time Lexxy was supposed to meet with Lucky, and he had been blowing her phone up, but she didn't want to answer while Carley was driving, not until they got to the location. She didn't want Carley trying to get the upper hand on her.

When they walked into the house, there were chairs everywhere. This was a place Dutch used often when he held people hostage or for ransom, which Lexxy knew about, and she would use it for the same thing.

Zeke walked in front of Lexxy and Carley in front of him until Lexxy told them to stop.

"Now, tie up the boy."

"Lexxy, please let him go. He doesn't have anything to do with this."

"He has everything to do with this. What makes you so special that you get to keep your son, and I lost my child at the hands of you? A child for a child I think."

Lexxy let out a maniacal laugh, and it was the strangest thing ever. This entire time, Carley thought Lexxy was weak, and that she wasn't the type to go hard, but that was where she was wrong.

Once Carley realized she wasn't playing, she decided to tie Zeke up in one of the chairs with the ropes that were stained in blood on the floor. She couldn't believe she'd been caught slipping. How could she have let this happen?

When she was done, Lexxy pushed her down into the seat next to Zeke and tied her up. Her wrists were tied tightly behind her where her arms were stretched far in an up position.

An hour had now gone by, and Lexxy was ready to call Lucky.

"Now, since you thought you were going to hurt me and get away with it, I'm gonna hurt you, and I can hurt you way worse than you can hurt me."

"What are you gonna do? You might as well just kill me!"

Carley didn't know it, but she was going to die, that day, no matter what.

"Oh, I'ma kill you, but first, let's make a phone call."

Lexxy dialed Lucky's phone number and put it on speaker phone. Though Lucky was upset that she hadn't made it to their "date" yet, he was just happy to hear from her. He'd been sitting in the same spot waiting for her to show up.

"Lexxy, baby, where you at? I've been here for an hour."

Carley's face read confusion and anger, and that was exactly what Lexxy wanted to see.

"Lucky, I'm sorry, something came up. No, scratch that, let me just be honest, I set you up. There are things you don't know about your little Carley. She helped to kidnap me and then she beat my

baby out of me. Now, I have your son here with us. I'll allow you to come and pick him up, but Carley is mine."

Lucky was quiet on the other end of the phone, but Carley was screaming begging for Lucky to come and save her.

"He ain't comin' to save you, if he knows what's good for him. He won't leave here alive if he tries. Lucky, what you gon' do? You comin' to get your kid or what?"

Lucky thought about it, and this was the first time Lexxy had ever lied or deceived him. He did love Carley, but not in that way, not in the way he loved Lexxy. He didn't even know she was pregnant. He wished it would've been with his baby, but it wasn't. This was a major wake up call for him. He'd spent so much time pining over Lexxy that he was blind to the person he was living with. He knew Carley was crazy, but he didn't know she was this type, and it was all his fault, at least that's what he thought, and it was true, it did have a lot to do with him. Carley would've never wigged out the first time at the wedding if it weren't for Lucky.

"Yeah, I'll come get him. Send me the address, and Lexxy?"
"Mhmm?"
"I'm sorry, I really am. I'm sorry for all the problems my actions have caused. I'm so, so sorry."
"Don't mention it. My problem ain't with you. Come and get your son."

Lexxy ended the call. She could feel her insides becoming mushy. Her conscience was trying to tell her to stop what she was doing, but she didn't want to stop. She was going to see this through to completion.

Carley was now crying, scared and ashamed. Not

only was she going to lose her man, but her son was going to see her die at the hands of the woman whose life she tried to ruin.

"You have any last words to say to your son? I'm not an animal, I'll at least let you say goodbye."

Carley went over to Zeke and untied him. She sent Lucky the address and took a few steps back. She didn't get a chance to even have her child, but Carley did, and she wanted her son's face to be the last happy moment she had. She would at least grant her that wish.

Zeke was trying not to cry, but he knew from the moment he got in the car that nothing good was going to come of this moment.

"I, I'm scared, Mommy," Zeke mumbled.

Lexxy wasn't stupid. She knew if she didn't tie Carley up, she might get loose, and who knew what would happen? Lexxy grabbed the rope, steadying the gun in one hand and the rope in the other, and made Carley wrap the rope around her wrists. Lexxy pulled on them to make sure they were extra tight before she could have her moment with her son.

Carley's hands were tied, so she couldn't hold Zeke, but she put her head against his neck, trying to comfort him. "Don't be scared, baby. Your daddy is on the way to get you. You'll leave with him, and everything will be ok."

Zeke knew everything wasn't going to be ok. He knew in his soul that his mother was going to die.

"Be a good boy for Mommy, ok? Do your school work, and don't give Daddy, Uncle Quentin, or Uncle P a hard time, got it? Promise me."

"I promise, Mommy."

"You be Mommy's good boy, like I taught you, and don't you ever forget how much I love you."

From the side of the room, Lexxy wanted to feel bad for Zeke, but she was still hurting very badly, so she didn't know if she could feel bad. If anything, she was still feeling crazy.

But strangely enough, even through her crazed anger, she knew she had to let the clean up crew know where she was so they could come and clean up the mess once she was done.

She sent them a quick text letting them know where to meet her. She figured the job would be done by the time they got there, so she wasn't worried about time. As soon as she hit send, there was a knock at the door, and of course, it was Lucky.

Lexxy opened the door and let him come in. His eyes were instantly fixed on his son. Zeke's arms were wrapped tightly around Carley's neck, and she was telling him to leave.

"You gotta go with Daddy now, baby. Go ahead."

"No! I don't want to leave you!"

Carley looked at Lucky, and with pleading eyes, she moved her head towards Zeke, signaling for him to come and get him.

"Come on, kid. It's time to go," Lucky said with his head down. In that moment, even he was afraid of Lexxy. He'd never seen her look like this before.

"Please, I don't want to leave Mommy. Please, Daddy!"

"Zeke, I said let's go!"

Lucky walked over to Zeke and pried his small fingers, one by one away from Carley.

Zeke kicked and screamed, crying and all, and even in that, Lexxy's heart was still broken for her own child for her to care about the next kid.

Lucky picked Zeke up, and he collapsed in his arms crying.

Lucky didn't have time to say anything else to Lexxy; he just wanted to get his traumatized son out of there.

When he left, the door closed, slowly showing Carley the last image she'd ever have of her son.

"Now that they're gone…."

Lexxy wasn't going to just shoot Carley, no, she was going to beat her ass the way she had been beat. Lexxy put her gun down and started wailing on Carley, landing punch after punch against her face and the side of her head. Though she screamed in the beginning, she didn't have the energy to yell anymore. Her voice had finally been silenced. Lexxy's wedding ring was so sharp, when she hit Carley against the head, it made blood squirt out of her head.

Some of the blood even got on Lexxy's face, and that only made her punch harder.

Carley was now on the floor, still tied very tightly to the chair, and Lexxy was stomping her, over and over again.

When she realized Carley couldn't take any more, she knew her job was over. Lexxy grabbed her gun, her hair strewn all over face, hands sore and shaking with bloody knuckles, and she looked at Carley and said, "Don't you just wish you would've thought about what you were going to do before you did it? This could have gone so much differently. It didn't have to be like this."

Carley didn't move, and Lexxy knew she was probably dead, but just to make sure, she let off three bullets into her body, finishing the job if it wasn't done already.

Lexxy took several deep breaths, and she felt like she could finally breathe, like the pain she had was gone, and she left the house.

When Lexxy got back to her own house, it was late in the afternoon, and Cocaine was waiting for her on the porch steps. Before she came home, she stopped at a gas station and got a water bottle to clean herself off with. She had to ditch her hoodie in the house because it smelled like death, had blood on it, and gun powder from her rendezvous with Carley.

She pulled down her car mirror and looked at herself in the mirror. She still had a crazy look on her face, but she wasn't going to be able to make that go away so easily, so she chalked it up and got out of the car, ready to go straight in the house. Lexxy had her hands in her pockets as she walked up the stairs. Her knuckles were badly bruised, and her hands hurt something awful.

"Hello, wife. What you been up to?" Cocaine asked as he grabbed her arm when she tried to just breeze past him.

"Just taking some me time, you know, clearing my mind."

"I see, and how you do that?" Cocaine asked inquisitively.

"You know, just riding around, thinking."

"Mmm…that's funny. Look, let me show you something."

Cocaine pulled out his phone and scrolled to a text message and showed it to Lexxy.

"Hey boss, we're on our way to the location Lexxy sent. Just wanna know before we get there in case we need extra hands, is it just a body, or are we looking at a car and the house?"

Lexxy was caught red handed, and there was nothing she could do to hide it.

"So, what's that about? What body, baby? You do something you wanna tell me about?"

"Not in particularly," Lexxy said quickly.

"Well, whether you wanna tell me or not, you need to. We ain't got no secrets, Sexy Lexxy. Tell daddy what you did."

Lexxy rolled her eyes, annoyed with everything. She was mad that the clean up crew even said something to Cocaine. This was her doing, her body, her quest, and they blabbed about it, even though they didn't know that was what they had done. She didn't think she had to tell them to keep their mouths shut, but now, she realized she should have.

"It ain't no secret, I just didn't wanna talk about it, but since you're pressuring me, I guess I'll tell you. The body is Carley's. I had to get her back. I needed that release. She killed my baby, so I killed her."

Lexxy said it so nonchalantly, Cocaine couldn't believe it. He knew she had a little crazy in her, but he wasn't sure that he would ever see it.

"Mhm…well, you know I'ma have to tell Quentin, right? I don't want him unleashing his anger on innocent people because of something you did, and we need to be ready for a problem."

"A problem? Them niggas can get it just like she did, and the way you made it seem, he wants to be a part of this family so bad, I doubt he'll have anything to say. I honestly don't give a damn, Cocaine. She deserved what she got, and I'm not going back on it, period."

"I'm not saying you should. I'm not even mad. I feel where you comin' from, baby. I'm just letting you know in case the shit hits the fan. Where you do it at, and how?"

Cocaine was proud of Lexxy. He didn't want to say it because he didn't want to look like a killer, even though he was, but to Lexxy, he was just her husband, her man. He had his ways that she knew about, but still.

"Come in the house and take a shower with me; I'll tell you while we're in there."

"You ain't gotta tell me twice with your fine ass."

This was the closest Cocaine had come to sexual activity with her, and it was as close as he was going to get. Lexxy wasn't cleared for having sex, and he didn't want her little pussy to get infected because he was gon' let off another round of kids in her.

Together, they went into the house, took a shower,

and enjoyed it while talking about what she'd done to Carley and how she was able to pull it off with the help of Lucky.

"Girl, I'm so proud of you, look at my baby, the shoota."

Lexxy laughed and hit Cocaine in the arm. Hopefully their troubles would be over, and they could all go on happily.

L ater on that night, Cocaine wondered about Quentin and Paul and wondered if they knew about Carley. He figured Lucky wouldn't really know what to say or what to tell either of them, so he figured he'd make the call himself. He didn't want Lexxy doing it because she was still in rare form and would have no remorse whatsoever, not that they deserved any, but this was how the game went. It wasn't like she killed Carley because she felt like it. Carley wronged her and did her an injustice, so she was just getting her payback.

Cocaine slid out of bed and went into the bathroom to make the call. He suddenly felt like he had to shit, so he figured he'd do both while he was on the toilet.

"What up? You thought about what I said?" Quentin had text Cocaine his actual number earlier that day in case he decided to call him, so he was able to easily reach him.

"Yeah, so here's the thing, you know some shit can't be let go, and a part of that is Lexxy losing our baby. Because of that, she took a life for a life. Your sister ain't comin' home."

Quentin took a deep breath. He knew something like this happening was a possibility, but he didn't think it would happen so quickly. He assumed they'd have more time, that they'd even be able to say goodbye, but that wasn't the case. It wasn't going to happen, and now, it was too late.

Quentin had Cocaine on speaker phone, and Paul heard everything he said. Even though they knew eventually this would probably happen, it still hurt to know that their baby sister was dead.

"Charge it to the game, homie. She played a dangerous game; she had to know this shit was comin' for her," Paul said, announcing his presence.

"True."

They sat silently on the phone—no one knew what to say, but Cocaine remembered the conversation he had with his father and mother that morning, and he figured now was a good time to say something.

"So look, I talked to Moms, and she said she was cool with meeting y'all. I'ma give y'all one chance, one chance to prove yourselves, that's it. If you betray me, my trust, or this family, I'ma have to go ahead and kill y'all. We all understand each other, right?"

"Yeah, we got it."

They disconnected the call, and Cocaine went on to take his shit.

Meanwhile, back at Quentin and Paul's house, Quentin's devastation hit him harder than he thought it would, and he couldn't help but cry, but even in his tears, there was only one thing he wanted to do: unite the families together.

"I know you don't wanna hear what I'm 'bout to say, but I'ma say it anyway. For years, we been figthin' with the Gorilla Gang when we didn't have to. We all family, and we could've been living like we were this whole time, and I want that. I want the family."

"You want a family you don't even know. This nigga Cocaine got yo' mind rocked. It don't make no sense. I can't do it, bro. I can't stand by you while you do some shit," Paul said honestly. He didn't give a damn about the family. Quentin was plenty family for him.

"I pretty much raised you. I took care of you. You've always been like my child, but you gon' choose this imposter of a brother over me? You gon' choose somebody else over me?"

Quentin didn't understand why his brother didn't get what he was trying to do, what he wanted to do. Together, they could unite the gangs and do something none of them had ever been able to do, reunite the streets. There would be no more fighting, no more bloodshed, they could live their lives and actually have real lives to live.

"I'm not choosing anybody over you; I'm putting family first, and if you don't want to accept it, that's on you, but we supposed to put family first. We always thought we were the only family we had, but now, we got an extension of a family that could change the world for us. I don't wanna be warring against you, so either you with me, or against me. If you against me, I'll cut my losses and do what I gotta do. If you with me, then you gon' be willin' to help me. You're my brother, and you've taken care of me my whole life. I love you, bro, but it's time."

Paul shook his head and thought about it. He loved his little brother and hoped that this wasn't some type of trick from the enemy. He wanted to be able to trust his brother, but he was very immature, and he wasn't too bright, but he had passion, and Paul knew no matter how hard he tried, he couldn't kill that passion. He couldn't take that light away from him.

"Listen, I got your back. Whatever you wanna do, I got you. For once, I'ma follow your lead, but first, we gotta bury our sister, and then we can do what we need to do."

Quentin thought about Carley and how he didn't want to end up like her. He knew there more than likely wouldn't be a body because he knew how this shit went, but they would still have a memorial service for her for the people who cared about her.

The next day, Quentin and Paul went to put together a service for their sister, and while they were there, for some reason, an idea hit Quentin that he knew would help prove their allegiance to Cocaine and his family.

"P, why don't we give Dutch to them? They don't know where this nigga is at, and I know they gotta be lookin' for 'em. He came to us to help, so he was definitely trying to get away from them."

Paul stroked his chin and gave some thought to what Quentin was saying. He didn't want to get his hands dirty with this, but he told his brother that he wanted to help and that he had his back, so he would go along with the plan and make some shit shake.

"I'm wit' it. However you wanna go about it. Whatever you wanna do it. I'm there."

"Cool."

Quentin began planning out the greatest killing to

have ever gone on. He would be the one who suggested a way to restore peace and balance, and Cocaine would have no choice but to accept him, to take him in, and let him finally meet his mother.

Quentin called Cocaine and put him up on game, letting him know the plan he was thinking about.

"Nigga, that just might do it," 'Cocaine said, amused with his plan. He truly was. He'd been wanting Dutch all these years, and now, he and his father would be able to put this nigga out of his misery, and the revenge that started it all would be over.

"Aight, so here's what we gon' do…"

Quentin's plan was fool proof, and as he said it to Cocaine, his dick began getting hard; it throbbed even. He wondered what he would do once his purpose was fulfilled. Would he be able to live a regular life? To go on and be a family man? Part family man, part king pin?

That didn't even matter now. He was finally going to take back his power, and his father would be restored as the true king of the Gorilla Gang.

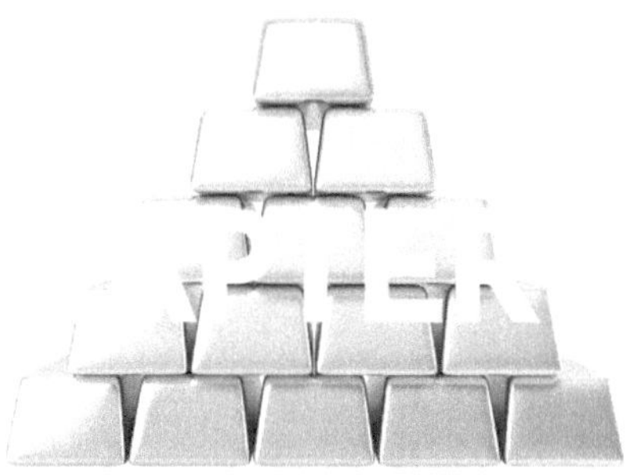

Though there was no body to bury, Quentin and Paul still laid their sister's memory to rest in the family's tomb, where the things she treasured most would still be with family, and Zeke would always have a place to come to so he could feel connected to his mother.

It took four days for them to get her service together, and it was nice, but the time for mourning was over, and the time to move on was upon them. Paul told Quentin that he'd gotten soft, so in order to set Dutch up, he was going to have to be the one to even suggest them leaving the house. Since they'd been keeping Dutch, giving him sanctuary, Dutch refused to leave the house. He was paranoid that if he left, someone would spot him, and somehow, it would get back to Cocaine or even Juaqeen.

Though Dutch knew that Jayla had been rescued with the help of Cocaine, he didn't know that Juaqeen played a part in it. Quentin was glad he never mentioned it, or else he would've never trusted what they were about to say. He would've smelled the deceit on their breaths.

That morning, Paul waited until Dutch came down for his morning coffee and the newspaper. He waited until he heard him coming down the stairs, and then they acted as planned.

"Man, we gotta get them niggas, and we doin' it today! You think I'ma let them get away with killin' our sister, and we ain't gon' retaliate? Them entitled mothafuckers!" Paul yelled, slamming his fists against the table.

Dutch, who was a nosey Rosy, heard what was going on and wondered what they were talking about.

"Shit, me too. That's why I got the Lischey Mob on stand by ready to take them niggas down. All we gotta do is meet them at the spot. Cocaine thinks he's good, living life happily, but that shit ends today. The Lischey Mob is ready to go, so hurry up and get yo' shit together, it's time for take off!" Quentin agreed.

"Mmm….do I hear a devious plot?" Dutch asked as he picked up the newspaper.

"Hell yeah, we 'bout to go shoot it out with them niggas. They think they can just take Carley from us and it won't be no blow back? They crazy as fuck, why? You tryna get in on the action?" Paul asked as he rose from the table.

Dutch thought about it, and with the help of the Lischey Mob, they could definitely take Cocaine down. He knew to probably expect Wild Bill, and maybe a few others, but as long as they were outnumbered, he felt confident that this would be easy enough. He'd been waiting to see Wild Bill again anyway to kill his ass, to take him out of this world for all the shit he'd done to him, for siding with the enemy over him.

"Where are they? How'd y'all set this shit up?" Dutch asked, wondering how he was able to make something like this happen. This was the only part Quentin and

Paul hadn't thought about, but Paul was quick on his feet, and he knew how to tell a believable lie.

"We been havin' a tale on them, following their every move. Them niggas just moved, and we've been keeping tabs on them from day one. Them niggas is actually bold enough not to have no security around the house."

"No security?" Dutch asked.

"Shit, not unless that Bill nigga counts as security. It's been the same four of them together at all times, so now is the time to strike before they get smart and wise up on us."

Dutch nodded his head. He was so full of himself that he really believed this. All of his paranoia had been for nothing. Here he was thinking that they were out to get him, when it seemed that they had their focus on something else.

"So what's up, you in, or you out?" Quentin asked, pretending to be fuming.

"Hell yeah, I'm wit' it. Let me grab my shit!"

Dutch was happier than a kid on Christmas. This was all he'd dreamed of since the day he met Cocaine. He would finally do what he did to his father, and there would be no one in the way of him and the Gorilla Gang. They'd have to pledge their whole allegiance to him. Since Lexxy wasn't his child, she had no real right to the gang, and she didn't want it anyway, at least she'd never expressed it before. She was always somewhere with her head in a book, and that was fine that that was the life she'd chosen, but this was what Dutch was born for. He was made for this life; Lexxy wasn't.

He felt bad for what Quentin and Paul had done to

her, but she was just a casualty in war that often happened. Hell, if his mother was still alive, he would throw her ass in the line of fire just to protect himself, and he didn't give a damn about Lexxy. The day she decided to side with the enemy, she chose her life, and she betray him. Besides, it wasn't like she was really his child anyway. That was what he told himself over and over again to feel better.

Dutch loaded his gun, assuming this was going to be easy, that he wouldn't need another or even a lot of ammunition. He'd save his bullets for Cocaine; that was who he wanted anyway.

Though the three of them left the house together, they couldn't have been on more different pages.

"Alright, if we do this, we do it as a family. Anybody who doesn't want to take part should leave now. I don't know why all of y'all are here anyway."

Cocaine, their fearless leader was assembling the family, seeing who was really about it and who wasn't. Everyone was there except Ella Mae and of course Denise.

"Well, you know I ain't leavin'. I been waitin' on this moment for almost sixteen years, kid, so I'm stayin'."

"Me too," Roman said as he lit his cigar.

"I'm standing by you till the wheels off," Lexxy proclaimed.

"This nigga and I been havin' beef since the

beginning of time. He always thought he was better than me and tried to keep me down. Now I got my life, my woman, and my daughter, and this nigga gotta go. I wanna be here for that," Wild Bill said.

"Shit, me too!" Junie didn't need to get into all the things he'd done to her. Everyone knew, and she didn't even want to bring it back up. She needed this so she and Wild Bill could finally get married since Dutch wouldn't sign the papers, the only way she would be free of him was if she became a widow.

Cocaine looked around at his family and couldn't believe how they were all willing to stand with him, but Dutch had offended all of them in one way or another, and it was time for them to finally get pay back.

It didn't matter how it happened; the fact that it was happening at all was the best thing in the world.

Wild Bill had never told anyone else about the second home he rented; it was something he planned to give to Junie after their wedding, but it would serve as Dutch's death place.

Cocaine kissed Lexxy on the lips, passion raging through the both of them. In another week or so, Lexxy was going to be able to have sex with her man, and when she finally could, she was going to release all of her love onto him.

Dutch, Quentin, and Paul pulled up to the front of the house, all of them itching for this plan to work out.

"Aye, the boys already got them in the house ready to get hit, you ready? This shit gon' be easy as fuck," Quentin lied. "All we gotta do is walk in, and all this shit will be over."

Dutch was so high and mighty, he had no idea that this was a set up.

Quentin, Paul, and Dutch got out of the car, guns ready to go. Quentin opened the door, and they walked straight in.

"Come on; they should be back here," Quentin said.

The three of them followed the hallway to the back of the house, where it turned into a large, enclosed patio.

Dutch's mouth watered, thinking he was about to get his revenge, when really, in actuality, he was about to meet his death.

They opened the door to the patio, and Quentin and Paul scooted to the left of the door, leading Dutch straight into the trap. Cocaine was standing to the right side of the door, ready to disarm Dutch as soon as he walked in.

Dutch didn't even think to look in the room before he stepped through the door; he just walked in, dressed like he was a real king. He had on a gold chain, black slacks, a black button down, and gold gators. He thought he was about to be recrowned king.

Pop!

Cocaine hit Dutch over the head with the butt of his gun, making Dutch stumble a bit.

Lexxy saw which direction he was falling in and grabbed the gun from his arm, rendering him defenseless.

Dutch finally caught his balance, and he turned around and looked at Quentin and Paul. He realized he'd been set up.

"So what, y'all gon' kill me? Who's gon' do it? Not you Lexxy; you ain't got the heart."

"That's where you're wrong. Who you think put Carley down? Me and me alone," Lexxy said coldly as she held the gun in his direction.

"I raised you, you little ungrateful bitch."

"Yep, and you lied to me my whole life, you weren't a parent. Looking back on it, I realize now just how terrible you were, and you deserve this. You deserve everything you're about to get, but I do wanna thank you. Without you, I would've never met Cocaine. I would have never fallen in love, and I'd still be somewhere waiting on Lucky's ass to change, so thank you."

From the dark shadows of the room, Juaqeen appeared along with Roman. As they approached him, Dutch began backing up, but there was nowhere for him to go. He'd run right into Paul and Quentin who pushed him back in their direction, and he fell face forward.

Juaqeen pulled his pants up so that his groin wouldn't be scrunched up in his pants, and he squatted down right in front of him, Roman laughing hysterically in the background, only adding to the thrilling experience.

"Long time no see, friend. How does it feel to know the one job you had, the one thing you were supposed to do, you didn't complete? You temporarily borrowed my life, but today, I'm taking that back, but you know, in the words of my daughter-in-law, I'm thankful for you too. If it wasn't for you, my son probably wouldn't be the man he is today, and he would've never met Lexxy, and who knows what could have happened to him, so thank you, my nigga."

Dutch couldn't believe this. All this talking was going on around him, and all he could think about was how this wasn't how you repaid gratefulness.

"If y'all muthafuckas is feeling so grateful, then why I gotta die?"

Wild Bill and Junie who had been in the bathroom fooling around like teenagers up until a minute or so before that, came into the room after hearing Dutch's voice.

"Oh no, you gotta go. I need my freedom. I need to be rid of the poisonous toxin you released into our lives years ago," Junie admitted. She knew even before the last year or so that Dutch was someone she didn't recognize. Over the years, he'd gotten even crazier and had become less of a father and husband, and more of a complete mobster. The heart that beat in his chest wasn't like it used to be, and Junie noticed that change even before then.

"You too?" Dutch asked as he watched Wild Bill slide his hand behind Junie's back and around her waist.

"Shit, let's just be honest, everybody in this room has a problem with you, and everyone in this room is going to take part in this."

There was nothing more for Dutch to say. He was in a position that he couldn't get out of, and though he wanted to pray and ask God for forgiveness, he didn't even really believe in God. He didn't believe that even if there was one up there, that he'd be forgiven anyway.

"But I ain't gon' die on the ground like an ani—"

He never got to finish his sentence. One by one, they all lined up to take their shots. Junie was the first one to fire off into his belly, then Wild Bill behind her, in the leg, Roman followed behind him with a shot to the arm, and Lexxy, she wanted to shoot him with his own gun, but she figured Juaaeen and Cocaine deserved the honors of doing that. She checked the chamber and saw that there were three bullets inside. That was perfect.

Lexxy wanted to shoot him, but she also wanted him to feel what she was going to do to him personally. Though his mistake brought her a true love, it also ruined a part of her life. Dutch was the reason for all the good and bad things that had happened to her lately, and it was time that he paid.

Lexxy whipped a knife out of her pocket, and she looked him in the eyes. This was the hardest man to kill. He was still hanging on, just barely, but hanging on nonetheless. Lexxy bent down and whispered something chilling in his ear.

"After today, no one will ever speak about you or even remember you. Your legacy dies here. With no children, no wife, no friends, you'll die alone, around the people who loved you most, and that you could have had a family with."

And with those last, bold words, she lifted her knife, and dug it deep into his chest, right into his heart.

He groaned in pain, hoping he would die before Cocaine and Juaqeen got their chance, but he was too strong to just die like this.

"Here Dad, you first," Cocaine said as he took the gun and handed it to his father.

"Nah, son, you go ahead. You went your whole life, waiting for this moment. I ain't gon' rob you of it today."

Cocaine was being polite, but if his father was going to let him deliver the final blow to Dutch, he wasn't gon' keep arguing about it. Cocaine cocked the gun and pulled the trigger, landing a bullet directly in the center of his forehead, the shot that ended his life.

Though Juaqeen didn't have to, he shot Dutch anyway. He deserved it.

Juaqeen let off the last two bullets—one in his chest, and the other in his eye.

The man who started it all was finally dead, and they all felt a sense of relief that they'd done this as a family, together, the way it was meant to be.

Paul and Quentin had been standing off to the side. Paul wondered if Cocaine would really hold up his end of the deal, not for himself, but for his brother. He wanted to make sure that even after they did what they were supposed to do, that Cocaine wasn't on no snake shit, but Quentin was so surprised by what had taken place, he was speechless.

"Call the crew, tell them to come get this nigga, baby," Cocaine said as he wiped the blood from around his face that splattered up when he and Juaqeen shot Dutch.

Lexxy nodded her head and stepped into the other room to make the call. Cocaine walked over toward Paul and Quentin and stuck out his hand for them to shake.

"A deal is a deal," Cocaine said with a smile on his

face. He was surprised they actually came through, and now, Cocaine didn't even want to kill them; he was proud of them, but he should've known, they were family after all.

Cocaine opened the other door on the other side of the room, and out walked Jayla. She wore a lightweight jogging suit with Adidas. She was dressed to run for just in case this somehow went south.

When she entered the room, it was like they were in the presence of a queen. Jayla had endured the most pain and suffered at the hands of her own children, and because of Dutch and Amir, she had gone through some of the worst moments in her life, but she wanted to forgive her children, to accept them and take them in, to love them the way they deserved to be loved.

Quentin's breath caught in his throat, his chest tightening around his airway.

Jayla stood there with her arms open, waiting to embrace them.

Quentin couldn't take it anymore; his heart was tearing at the seams, and he just wanted his mother. He wanted to apologize, to tell her he didn't know. There wasn't a dry eye in the room. The moment was priceless and touching.

With her arms wide open, she feared rejection, the unknown of what might happen, but Quentin had been waiting on this moment his entire life, and he wasn't going to waste it with what if's.

He almost ran into her arms, letting her cradle him like a baby.

"I'm sorry, Mama. I'm so sorry," he cried into her shoulder.

"Shhh…it's ok. I know. I know."

She rocked him back and forth like he was a small child as an ocean of tears flowed down their bodies.

Jayla opened her other arm, wanting Paul to come in for a hug as well, but he was reluctant. He didn't realize it, but the feeling he'd been having this whole time was guilt. He felt guilty for the part he played, and Jayla knew it. She saw the look of hurt in his eyes, and there was only one way to set him free.

"I forgive you, Paul. I forgive you."

Paul didn't know it, but those were the words that he needed to subconsciously hear to let this all go, to accept his mother because he was actually having a problem accepting himself.

Though Paul was the oldest, and was definitely the strongest, in this moment, he became weak. Weak for his mother, for the family he secretly yearned for.

The distance between Paul, his mother, and his brother were now closed as he too joined in their embrace, feeling the love he'd been missing his entire life.

Cocaine seeing the love and also feeling it, came in to engulf the three of them with his long arms.

These were his brothers and a great addition to their family.

"I guess y'all proved yourselves," Cocaine said as they all laughed.

Lexxy was so happy. They got their revenge, they had their family, and now, they would be able to truly live happily ever after.

"You a reflection of me, shawty. You a reflection of me," Moneybagg Yo's *Reflection of me* blasted through the speakers as Ella Mae and Roman's new house filled with family and friends alike. Roman couldn't keep staying with his grandson. He'd spent too much time away from his woman that she was the only person he wanted to be around, and there was no way he was going back to Haiti. He made sure his clients got the last bit of work they would ever get from him as he was retiring, and he had his things moved into his new home with his woman.

Roman was throwing the whole family a party for all they'd gone through and for everything they'd accomplished, and it was a smash hit.

Cocaine and Lexxy were happy and together, Junie and Wild Bill had gone to the courthouse and gotten married. They didn't want a big wedding since they were older, which ended up turning into a double wedding. The statute of limitations on a faked death were over for Jayla, so she was able to live a free life the way she wanted, and she'd finally become Mrs. Blackwood.

This was the first time Lexxy had seen Denise in forever, but she understood why her best friend couldn't be around. She didn't really want her involved in all the drama they had going on anyway.

Denise came in with her red palazzo pants, pink hair swinging from side to side, and a bandeau top that fit her breasts perfectly. In her hands, she held a large present.

Lexxy noticed Denise immediately. She commanded attention when she walked into any room, and today was no different.

"Bestie!" Lexxy yelled as she ran and jumped on her. "You look beautiful."

"So do you. I see ya' little booty pokin' out. Let me find out you gettin' thicker because of that good dick you gettin'."

Cocaine heard Denise from across the room, being fresh and bold as always. He glared at her, and she bust out laughing. She and Cocaine had a brother and sister relationship, and she loved making him feel uncomfortable.

"Come on, I want you to meet somebody."

Lexxy pulled Denise's arm through the crowd, and when they stopped, they were at a table where there were all types of liquor being poured and a heavy card game going on between Wild Bill, Junie, Juaqeen, and Jayla. Quentin and Paul were standing behind Jayla, trying to tell her what cards to play since she'd never played Phase 10.

"This is the most intense game I've ever seen!" Denise said, picking up a shot of Bourbon and throwing it back.

"This is Quentin and Paul, Quentin, Paul, this is my best friend, Denise."

Paul's eyes were instantly glued to Denise. He'd never seen anyone who he thought was that pretty, nor did he know a woman alive who could take a shot of Bourbon straight to the head and keep rolling like she'd drank water.

"Hey, what up?" Quentin said, not paying attention to her.

"Hey, how you doin'?" Paul asked as he came around the back of Jayla to meet Denise.

"I'm good, how are you?"

"I'm coolin', watchin' Moms lose this damn game." he chuckled.

"She must be losing because of you, look at how well she's playing now." Denise pointed to the table where Jayla was now smacking cards down, killing Phase two.

"Damn, maybe you right. We can't all be good luck charms, I guess."

Denise blushed and shrugged her shoulders. This was what Lexxy wanted. Denise had a great life, but she didn't have anyone to share it with, and she'd endured a lot of the pain they all carried. Lexxy wanted her happiness almost as much as she wanted her own.

"I'ma let you two get acquainted, I'll be back," Lexxy said, and then she walked away. The truth was, she wanted to get a taste of her man, and tell him some good news.

She found Cocaine and grabbed his hand, taking him upstairs. Lexxy closed and locked the door behind her and jumped on the bed.

"What's going on?" Cocaine asked, curious as to what was going on.

"You and me."

Lexxy began undressing, stripping all the way down to nothing. It had taken her some time to get comfortable with the permanent bruising she had from being down in that basement, but Cocaine always kissed and caressed her entire body, letting her know she was still the most beautiful woman in the world to him.

Lexxy moved her finger in a come here motion, and he got into the bed next to her.

"I wanna show you something," she whispered.

"I wanna see whatever you tryna show me, Sexxy Lexxy. Fucking in my granddaddy's house, you nasty," he responded seductively.

Lexxy reached over in her nightstand and pulled out a pregnancy test.

"Seriously? Already?"

"Mhmm…a month and some change."

Cocaine couldn't believe this. Well, he could because he was dicking his wife down every chance he got, but he was surprised because the doctor said it would be hard for her to carry a baby because of the trauma she'd experienced to her uterus.

"And how do you feel about this?" Cocaine asked, truly caring about her feelings.

"Honestly, I'm over losing the first baby. It hurt, true enough, and I've never been in more pain in my life, but things are different now. We're a happy family, and I think it's fine. I got pregnant again for a reason, and I don't think we've come this far to lose it all, and besides,

I'm ready to be a mother, more so now than before, and as badly as I want to be a doctor, I've been in the hospital enough in this lifetime, I'm over it. I think I just want to take some money and invest in a medical group."

"I think that's a good idea, my queen. Now that the Gorilla Gang and the Lischey Mob are together, thanks to Paul and Quentin, I think it's safe to say, the streets are safe, our home is safe, and our family is protected. But you know what I be thinkin' 'bout all the time though?" Cocaine asked Lexxy as he ran his fingers up her bare thighs.

"What's that?" Lexxy responded, chills going through her body.

"What would've happened if you were still with that nigga Lucky. If you'd be with that square instead of a real nigga like me."

"Nah, I'd never choose a square over a hood nigga. Let's just be honest, dopeboys do it better."

Cocaine laughed and climbed on top of his beautiful wife, and there was nowhere else in the world he'd rather be. All of the drama and chaos that led to this moment was worth it in his eyes.

He was on his way to having a baby, he had his father, grandfather, grandmother, and mother all in the same place.

This shit was like cake with fifty layers of icing on it.

Cocaine and Lexxy made love all the way through the party and finally got up when they heard people leaving. They tried to straighten the bed back up the best they could, but those sheets were laid before they got in there, and now, they were tragic, but Roman would understand; he was a freak himself.

Cocaine and Lexxy walked hand and hand downstairs, where she could see Denise cuddled up on the couch with Paul, Quentin was in the corner talking to one of Lexxy's friends from the hospital, Sha, and their family was being loud, enjoying themselves.

The day couldn't have gotten any better.

Four years later.…

"Come on, now. Get your suit on CJ. 'Lexiana, where are your stockings? I know I took this stuff out for you last night," Lexxy said to her beautiful twins who were running around their home acting like little chickens with their heads cut off.

Four years had passed, and the drama had subsided. The Blackwood family was whole, and brighter days followed.

Cocaine came into their bedroom, dressed, looking sexy, chocolate dripping from his body like a fondue fountain.

"Cocaine, get your kids. I can't get them dressed, Lexi's stockings are missing, this can't be happening today."

"Slow down, woman. I got this. Go finish getting yourself ready; Denise will be pissed if we're late or if we miss her wedding because you weren't even ready. Let's go, maid of honor."

Cocaine smacked her on the butt and finished getting the kids ready. Their children were just as chocolatey as they were, beautiful from head to toe, and they were spoiled beyond reason.

Thirty minutes later, the kids were ready and so was Lexxy, so they could finally go.

Denise had fallen madly in love with Paul, courtesy of Lexxy, and he'd finally asked her to marry him last year, and they'd taken their time, seeing what it would be like for them to live together, their habits, and to build a real friendship, but now, Denise was going to tie the knot with him.

When Cocaine and Lexxy made it to the church, Lexxy grabbed the kids' hands and pulled them inside so they could get comfortable with Junie and Wild Bill. Cocaine was a groomsman, and Lexxy was the maid of honor, so they needed to get in place before the ceremony went down.

On their way to the back to meet with Denise, Paul, Quentin, and Sha who had worked her way into the family by dating Quentin, Lexxy noticed several blacked-out cars in front of the church.

"Do you see that, baby?" Lexxy asked Cocaine as he looked in the direction of where her eyes were glued.

"Yeah, it's probably just security for the wedding. You know Paul is paranoid as fuck that somebody is always out to get him, even though we've been living in peace for years."

"Better safe than sorry, I guess." Lexxy shrugged the nagging feeling she had in her belly off and continued going to the back to be with her best friend.

Cocaine kissed Lexxy as he met with Quentin and

Paul in the hallway and said, "I'll see you in a minute, beautiful. You look amazing."

"I know I do." Lexxy smirked and continued on her way.

The wedding was underway, and Lexxy and Cocaine came down the aisle first, and then Quentin and Sha. Quentin was amazed by how easily their lives all changed and how their relationships had grown in the last couple of years.

Lucky had taken Zeke and moved him back to Chattanooga where he could be close to Carley's mother and his grandmother. Paul and Quentin missed him terribly, but he understood that Lucky was doing what was best for his family.

After all the dirt Paul and Quentin had done in their lives, they never believed they'd have a happy ending, but here they were, just seconds away from it.

Though Paul and Quentin were Amir's children, Jayla was their mother, and their loyalty was to her above all, so they dropped their last names, and Juaqeen legally adopted him as his children, and they joined the Blackwood family as well.

Even as adults, they needed a male role model in their lives, and who better than the great Juaqeen?

Denise's wedding song, *I'll Be Loving You Forever* by Westlife came on, and she began walking down the aisle, ready to join the Blackwood family too.

Denise didn't bother inviting her father to the wedding; she honestly wanted nothing to do with him, so she came down alone, smiling, and just as happy as she would've been with an escort.

The church doors that had been closed suddenly flew open, and everyone in the church turned around.

"Ladies and gentleman, we ask that you all remain seated while we conduct this arrest."

"Arrest?" Denise yelled as she looked at the ten men in front of her with all black suits on.

"Yes ma'am. Juaqeen Blackwood, Roman Blackwood, Cocaine Blackwood, Paul and Quentin Blackwood, you all are under arrest for the murders of Dutch Hassle, Carley Boden, and Leon Jessup. Also, for Racketeering, and human trafficking. You have the right to remain silent…"

As one of the officers read them their Miranda rights, Cocaine's mind went back to a strange time, where he remembered Leon. Why would they think they had anything to do with Leon's death? He was family, and none of them would have ever hurt him. It had been years since they'd seen him, but Cocaine didn't think he was dead. Human trafficking? They weren't into no shit like that, and why were they throwing all of these charges together on all of them?

"No!" Denise yelled as the officers began storming the church, heading to take the men down, and from the inside of the pit where the officers had disbursed, she saw a familiar face, and didn't understand.

"Daddy? What…what are you doing here?"

Weddings apparently weren't meant to be for the

Blackwood family, and as the men were torn away, Lexxy realized now, more than ever, she was going to have to boss up not only for her man, but for her entire family.

The Blackwoods wouldn't be going down without a fight, and Lexxy was damn sure ready to bring it.

"It's ok, baby. Call the lawyer, tell him everything that happened. I love you," Cocaine said as he tried yanking away from the officers.

"I'm calling now!" Lexxy went to the purse that her mother held. Alexiana and CJ watched their father be dragged away in cuffs. Though they were just babies, the feeling in the air of despair and confusion transferred onto them, washing over them like a bath that was way too hot. The babies were agitated and moving around, trying to get comfortable. Previously, they'd fallen asleep, but with all the commotion going on in their little baby worlds, they couldn't find their safe place, and it made them act up, cry and whine; weddings are not supposed to last longer than the babies' nap.

Lexxy noticed her children were becoming unruly and restless, but she couldn't focus on that right now. All she could see was her man being taken away from her, and her best friend's day being ruined. This was not supposed to be happening. With all the charges they were facing, shit was about to get nasty.

Four years of peace couldn't prepare them or even ok the fact that this was happening.

Lexxy stepped to the side and called their lawyer. Hopefully the boys would get bond; they had money, so getting them out wouldn't be an issue, but Lexxy wanted to know what they were looking at. A trial? More jail time? This day, Denise's special day, would forever be marked by tragedy, and possibly the day her man, her family, lost their freedom.

As the officers drug the Blackwood men out of the church, Paul dug his feet into the ground trying to stand before Denise one final time.

"You look beautiful, baby. I love you," 'Paul said through gritted teeth. Denise grabbed him just in time, before he was taken outside, and she planted the softest, most passionate kiss on him she could because she didn't know what was to come. She could only hope this would be over before anything worse happened.

Denise's father stood in the middle of the aisle, looking at his handywork. He'd never felt so proud of himself, but on his daughter's wedding day? How could he ruin her moment? It was supposed to be a father's pride and joy to walk his daughter down the aisle, to attend the wedding, but Denise had offered him neither. Was this all out of spite?

Outside, the church the boys were caravanned into separate cars, all black, with the letters F.B.I written boldly across one of the cars. They'd been caught by the feds, but how? Separated into two's, Paul was thrown into a car with Cocaine, Quentin was herded in with Juaqeen, but Roman was alone.

As the boys rode away to their fates, their minds were

all spinning. Roman was prepared for a day like this to come. He knew eventually, something like this would happen. In the profession he was in, death or prison were the only way out, and sometimes, those two came together. Though he didn't imagine he'd be an old man going out like this, but he was just glad to have had a good, long ride, and he had been reunited with Ella Mae, so he had no regrets, no losses, and he was happy with what his life.

"Don't say nothin' to them. Not without the family lawyer. Be cool," Cocaine coached Paul who was sweating bullets. He was more worried about Denise's day being ruined than he was going to jail. This wasn't his first run in with the law. He thought after he escaped the snares of the cops the last time seven years ago that that would be his last go round with them, but he was clearly mistaken. Though he'd only done a few days in jail the last time, he was one hundred percent afraid of going for any time longer. He wasn't made for jail. Paul liked to eat, and he loved his freedom; he loved being with his woman, and he looked to the future they'd have together, and now, that could be snatched away from him in the blink of an eye.

"I ain't sayin' shit," Paul said through clenched teeth.

Cocaine knew he was nervous, but he wouldn't let his brother go down. He didn't have any kids, a legacy to leave of his own. He would do anything he could to see his family out of this mess, even if it meant taking some trump charges just so they could get back to the women they loved. Yeah, Lexxy would be pissed, but she was a real rider. He knew she was built for this life, and she could handle it, handle it more than Denise and Sha who though they had been around the game, they'd never seen anything but its perks really. Denise had seen a few things, but even still, she'd never had to experience it herself.

"Paul, look at me," Cocaine said as he looked at his brother's face that was completely stricken with fear.

Paul looked at his brother, trying to hide what he felt inside.

"It's gon' be cool. Don't worry. They separated us to try to divide and conquer. They wanna see who's gon' flip on who, but they don't know the Blackwood family. They don't know what we come from."

Paul put his head down and mumbled, "We ain't all Blackwoods, bruh. We don't come from the same stock."

"Nah, but we come from the same struggle, and you a Blackwood too, nigga. Blood don't make us family, it makes us related. What makes us family is the bond we share, the same type of upbringing in the drug game. We come from the same type of family struggles. Daddy problems, mother abandonment issues, crazy females, fucked up lil' brothers. You family, man, don't trip."

Cocaine's words resonated loudly within Paul. Even though Juaqeen had adopted Paul and Quentin, sometimes, he still felt like an outsider because for him, he couldn't imagine something so good happening to him in such a small amount of time. He found the girl of his dreams, inherited a large family, found his mother, and a father, who though didn't spawn his DNA, was a father to him nonetheless, and whether Paul realized it or not, Juaqeen saw him no differently than he did Cocaine.

The officers got into their cars, mounting up with pride to drive the boys off to a place worse than any street corner they could ever face :the interrogation room.

Though the other officers were gone, Denise's father remained. Even through the chaotic church chatter, Denise's glare at her father was even louder than the wedding guests.

Angrily, she marched up the aisle toward her father, grabbing his jacket and pulling him to the back where her dressing room was. Her father's face had a grin so wide, the Joker's slashed lips didn't have shit on the happiness he felt.

"Daddy, what the hell are you thinkin'? Why would you do this to me?"

"Denise, look at you, you're beautiful, so beautiful, yet, you always fall for the wrong ones," Denise's father said sarcastically.

"Liam, I swear to God I could kill you. What is this? Just tell me, please!" Denise yelled, stomping her feet on the ground. To Liam, Denise was still his little girl, and she'd gotten herself into something that was even bigger than she was, and just like when she was a child, she'd throw a fit when she didn't get her way, and this was no different.

"I'd love to stay and chat, beautiful daughter, but I have to go. I got scum to put away. Call me later; we'll talk." Liam reached over and kissed Denise on the cheek and ran out of the door.

Denise's hand immediately went up to her face wiping off the kiss she'd been given by her father's slimy lips.

For this, no matter the reason, Denise would never forgive her father. There was nothing he could ever do to get back in her good graces, even though he'd fallen from them long ago.

Liam arrived at the F.B.I. headquarters in the middle of downtown Nashville in no time. This was a moment he'd been waiting on for the last fifteen years, something he'd been studying since he first was recruited as an agent.

Liam was at the top of his class in the police academy. He'd been hired on straight to the force, hitting the streets when he became a part of the local police department in Louisiana. He worked his way up to the task force, drug initiative program, and as he rose, he caught the attention of the F.B.I who Liam had assisted on several projects, just starting out.

The first week working with the F.B.I, he was praised, and most people were happy to have him as a part of the team, but the sad, sad truth was, there were also people above him who wanted to bring him down because he was "stealing" their shine, but he wasn't conceited. At one point, Liam was a regular, good man, until he received the case that would change his life and the world as he saw it.

His superior, Agent Jones, brought him a case file one day that read SENSITIVE across the top. This would be his first assignment, so it was already sensitive to him, but the words written across the folder in bold letters had nothing to do with his feelings and everything to do with the information on the inside.

The folder contained pictures of places, names, people's records, alias'—it was a tell-all book in just one very large folder with sub compartments.

Liam's sexual prowess was never stimulated by women alone; it was the bad guys that he dreamt of putting away that gave him a stiffy.

Liam opened the folder and began fingering the pages as if it was a woman; he enjoyed every moment of it. The first name he saw was Dutch's, and as he began combing through his file, he couldn't even think about any of the other information. He beat every charge to ever come against him, and as unlikely as something like that was, here it was, right in front of Liam.

After combing through all of the details in the file and looking into all of the names, he knew the one that would be easiest to penetrate was Dutch, though Juaqeen, Roman, and even Amir's names were inside the file as well. Dutch was the hardest fish to get anything to stick to, and Liam wanted him more than he wanted anything.

He committed to the job in its entirety by going under cover after a few years, and he had since been plotting against not only Dutch, but the entire Blackwood line. The feds were probably the only people in the world from Louisiana to Tennessee who wanted justice against the ever growing drug problem more than Liam. Liam moved Denise, enrolled her in the same school as Lexxy, and forced her into a friendship with her. After all, Lexxy was on the welcome committee at school, and the day Liam went to drop her off, when he saw Lexxy walking up to Denise, he knew he'd made a good decision. He parked his car and ran straight in after them.

"Dad, what are you doing?" a teenage Denise asked, almost embarrassed that her father came in the school. At this point, Denise thought her father was retired. He told her that he hated the force, and it took too much time away from her, but the truth was, since he was undercover, he could do anything, and he had. From time to time, he worked with the police on certain cases, just to lend a helping hand, but as far as Denise knew, her father worked from home with a security team that he managed. He'd gone to great lengths to create that cover, and even his own daughter believed it.

"I just wanted to see your new school. Looks like you've made a friend already."

"Hello, I'm Alexxus. Denise, is this your dad?" Lexxy asked as she extended her hand.

"Yes, Liam Ellis. It's nice to meet you. This is a nice school you all have here."

"Thank you. I certainly think so. I'm the head of the welcome committee, and it's an honor to have Denise. Would you like a tour of the school as well, Mr. Ellis?"

"Certainly. I'd love to see what the scholarship Denise was able to get through the police department is paying for." Liam was going

out of his way. Though he told Denise she was awarded a scholarship for the school, the truth was he was able to afford it himself, thanks to his salary at the Federal Bureau of Investigation.

"Follow me."

Lexxy led them around the entire school, showing them where her classes would be, all of which Lexxy was in, which Liam knew. He'd studied this family thoroughly, and he knew exactly where they were going because he knew the full-scale plan of the entire building.

"Well, Mr. Ellis, this is where we leave you. It's time for Denise to actually get to class."

"Absolutely, let me talk to Denise for just a moment."

"Of course, Denise, I'll see you in class."

Liam pulled Denise to the side. With her back against the locker, she stared at the empty hallways, wondering what she was doing here. Never in a million years did Denise think she would ever fit into a place like this. She was used to the poverish Louisiana schools where although it wasn't much to look at, she loved her school and her home, and she had a major since of pride of being there, and now, that was taken from her. The world she knew was ripped and torn away from her like a messy baby with ice cream.

"I think this place will be good for you. You should really try to get close to that Alexxus. She seems to know her shit, and it'll be a good opportunity to make new friends. I know that was one of your main concerns when leaving home, and now look at you, seems like you guys hit it off."

Denise rolled her eyes. Her father was pushing it. Denise had never really gotten along with girls; not because she didn't want to, but because most girls were intimidated by her nonchalant attitude when it came to boys and things most teenage girls thought of. Denise had a plan her entire life, and it never involved friends for the long run, not until she met Lexxy anyway. Hell, Denise was still a virgin, and hardly ever paid boys any attention anyway.

Liam noticed his daughter's hesitance, so he grabbed her arm lovingly, and said, "I know this is new. It's a big change for me, but sometimes, we just have to go with the flow and let life take us where we deserve to be. You deserve a better education than the one you were getting back at home. You deserve every opportunity to be given to you, and I'm glad I was able to give it to you. You're smart, Denise. Eventually, you'll see this was for the best."

Denise hated to admit it, but she knew her father was right. It was because of the dreams she had that she knew she needed a better education, that she needed to be around the right people to help her advance, so she took this new life and saw it as an opportunity to advance in the life she dreamt of having.

"Ok, Daddy, I'll give it a chance."

"Ah, atta girl! I knew you'd see reason in this. I love you, baby girl, have a good day."

Liam walked away from his daughter knowing that this was going to turn out the way he wanted. From that day on, Denise and Lexxy were inseparable, and Liam made sure that Denise and Lexxy stayed close; it was the only way he could get information. He never asked Denise any incriminating questions; he didn't want to lead on to the fact that he knew anything about Lexxy's family.

He instead stayed patient and watched all of their lives unfold around Denise's. Though he hated putting his daughter in harm's way, he hoped that if anything ever happened, he'd be able to get her out of it.

This case became his life, and it eventually enveloped and consumed him, thus bringing him back to this moment, where he'd been waiting to bust the Blackwood men.

Dutch's death was the straw that broke the camel's back, and Liam knew that he had to have all of his evidence, everything possible to take the boys down, and now, he had it. He had the missing pieces to the case that took over his life.

Liam walked into the first interrogation room, where Cocaine sat with a smile on his face. Though he never imagined anything like this happening, he knew how this was about to go. They were about to try and get him to talk, and Liam couldn't have been barking up a more wrong tree.

Cocaine was strong not only in body, but in his mental state, and he would never give away his family secrets, ever.

"Cocaine Blackwood, I've been waiting a very long time for this moment," Liam said as he took a seat across from Cocaine.

"And you gon' be waitin' even longer, 'cuz I ain't got nothin' to say to you."

"Defensive, that's good. Go ahead and get all that anger out. This is going to be a long day."

Liam propped his feet up on the table as he looked across at Cocaine. Not only was this day going to be long, but it would forever be marked in all of their minds. For some, this would end well, but not for everyone. The Blackwood men were strong, but for every strength, there is a weakness, and all of theirs were about to be played on.

The interrogation was getting nowhere, and Liam was becoming aggravated. He didn't want to have to coerce a confession out of him with pictures; he hoped Cocaine would give him something, anything to go on, but no matter the question, Cocaine denied, denied, denied. Cocaine said the magic words, "I want my lawyer," and Liam was forced to end the interrogation immediately, or else he'd be breaking the law, something he wasn't too fond of.

Even though he told Liam he wouldn't be answering any of his questions or giving anything up, and he wasn't, he wanted to know what all they had on the family, and Liam was stupid enough to fall for it. Based on his questions, Cocaine realized they indeed had solid evidence of the murders they'd been charged with, all except Leon's.

Leon raised Cocaine, treated him as if he were his father, and when Cocaine moved to Tennessee without a moment's notice, he left Leon behind, not because he wanted to but because he knew Leon would never approve of him making such a drastic move. Leon had always tried to steer him in the right direction, away from the drug life, which would only leave him with heart ache and pain, and even more so, against a lifetime of revenge, especially when there was nothing to get revenge for. Leon knew Juaqeen was alive, but that was something he'd promised himself he'd take to the grave to protect Cocaine, if only he'd been able to do so.

Cocaine left anyway, and over the years, he didn't forget Leon; he was just too embarrassed, too ashamed to reach back out to him. To his knowledge, Leon was fine. He found out at the wedding that he wasn't, and unfortunately, he didn't have time to mourn a man that was like a father to him because he was stuck in this room with Liam.

"You may think you're a tough nut to crack, but with the right amount of pressure, you'll fall apart."

Liam removed the folder he'd brought in with him from the table. It was previously sealed, and this was the first time even he'd seen the contents. He wanted this moment to be as real as possible, but the man in the authentication department assured him what the folder held would be more than enough to use to bring these guys down.

Liam began going through the folder, and an even wider smile invaded his lips. Some of the photos, he'd seen before, but thought they may not be real, and for the first time ever, his suspicions had been confirmed.

The first photo Liam smacked on the table, as if it were enough evidence to lock them all away. As soon as he slapped it onto the table, there was a knock on the door. Liam looked over his shoulder, and through the glass he could see it was a man with a briefcase and a bowtie tied so tight, it had to be strangling him. It was obviously Cocaine's lawyer.

Cocaine's smile turned into a smirk as he greeted his attorney and asked him to have a seat.

Liam looked over at Cocaine's attorney, and he could tell how well put together he was. He truly wasn't prepared for something such as this. Liam thought due to the sloppiness of some of the jobs that their representation would be just as bad, but he couldn't have been more wrong. The attorney recommended Cocaine keep his mouth shut, but Cocaine wasn't afraid of Liam. He'd already seen right through him, and he was prepared for whatever Liam was about to throw his way, hopefully.

"Do you remember this day?" Liam asked as he slid the photo across the table to a handcuffed Cocaine.

Cocaine looked at the photo, and though he was shook on the inside, he held his composure, and answered with a straight face.

"Yep, how could I forget? That was the day of our family barbecue."

"Family barbecue you say?"

"Yep, of course. The first one we ever had all together as a family."

"Mmm…and this? This doesn't seem like a family barbecue to me."

In the picture was Juaqeen and Cocaine standing over Dutch's dead body with smiles on their faces. The picture clearly showed everyone, and even still, Cocaine held his demeanor.

"Mmm…I'm not sure what you see, but I see a reason to celebrate. We all look so happy, see."

Cocaine would later regret saying that, but in this moment, he didn't give a damn.

"You do realize this is enough evidence to say that you're a guilty man, right?"

"Guilty to you. Twelve of my peers may not say the same thing," Cocaine said as he thought about his options. On one hand, he could confess to the murder and the rest of his family would be let go, at least he hoped they would. He could negotiate a deal if necessary, but on the other hand, he wondered how in the hell they even got this picture, and if there was a snitch amongst them, Cocaine couldn't afford to go to jail. Even though there had only been a few murders to come up, there were hundreds of other bodies left in all of their wakes. Lexxy had caught her first body, and he wouldn't dare let his baby go down. She killed Carley because the bitch deserved it, and Lexxy wasn't going to go down, not for something that could've all be prevented if it hadn't have even been for Dutch in the first place. It all always came back to him. Even in death this nigga was coming back to haunt them.

After realizing he wasn't going to get anywhere with Cocaine, something he should've realized from the beginning, but Liam was determined and assumed surely with that photo he'd be able to get a solid confession of some sort.

His next task was putting his foot down on Paul, who he assumed would be somewhat easier.

He tried again with the same photo.

"Paul Blackwood, Amir's son, recently adopted by Juaqeen Blackwood. I guess it's safe to say you have some serious daddy issues."

Paul wouldn't be easily intimidated. His brother had already prepared him for this on their ride over. He didn't know what they had against them, but no matter what was to come, there was no way he was going to let Liam get under his skin.

"No answer? Perhaps this will make you talk."

Again, Liam tried with the photo, along with a few others to make the blow hit even harder.

He placed both photos face up on the table, and Paul didn't have the same type of incognito skills that Cocaine had. Paul was shook but not because of what the average eye could see in the photos. To the far right of each one, there was a car parked in the backyard with someone inside of it.

The second picture was a photo of all of them in the room, standing there, looking at Dutch's dead body, including Lexxy, Jayla, and Junie.

Paul wondered what they had on them, and now he knew, and he knew exactly where it came from.

Paul wouldn't say anything to Liam, and he quickly asked for a lawyer. Using those words was a death trap to any officer of the law because of the right to proper representation.

"I ain't sayin' shit to you 'til my lawyer is present."

"Here's something you might want to think about; Denise is caught up in the middle of all of this, all of it. Wouldn't it be a shame to know that your own fiancé had something to do with sending you to prison for the rest of your life? That would be the perfect plot twist to this ghetto love tale, don't you think?"

Paul was handcuffed to the table, but that didn't stop him from trying to whoop Liam's ass. He began pulling at the chains, almost breaking his wrists he was tugging and pulling so hard, with so much force.

"Denise wouldn't do that to me. She loves me. She ain't no sell out like your ass, a nigga she didn't even bother to invite to the wedding. I know about you and your relationship; you was a shitty ass father, and that's why you missed the chance to walk her down the aisle. All those years she thought yo' ass was doin' security work, only to find out you a Fed. You a liar and a terrible ass father. So who got daddy issues now, nigga?"

Liam withdrew the pictures and left the room furious. He knew these guys would probably be lawyered up, but he thought, for some strange reason, that when Paul saw the picture with their entire family in the room, he'd confess, which couldn't have been further from the truth. Denise truly knew nothing about what was going on, and his tactics were weak as fuck. This only proved even more how terrible of a father he truly was to Denise. All the years he'd spent lying, and now he was going to try and make it seem as if she was the one who dropped the dime on them, when of course, that wasn't the case.

Denise loved the entire Blackwood family, not as if

they were family, but as family. They'd been there for her more than her own father was. She never knew her mother because that bitch was scandalous and ran away from her responsibilities as a mother.

When all of this was said and done, Paul just hoped he could get back to Denise in one piece. He still had every intention on making her his wife, no matter the outcome.

When they got engaged, he did something he never thought he would; he went and made a will, in case something ever happened to him, he thought it would be death, not this, but in the event something ever happened to him, Denise would have access to all the money, the connects, anything she could dream of, it would be hers, and he wanted that for her.

The last few years, Paul, Quentin, and Cocaine had done everything they could to start gong legit. Roman had invested a lot of his drug money in hotels, and so did they. They spread their money out amongst restaurants, hotels, grocery stores, and anything they could to wash their money, but that didn't stop them from their daily operations. They still had their trap houses, and the Gorilla Gang and the Lischey Mob were still in the streets, something they all were now regretting. They had more than enough money to do anything they wanted, and they should've taken their money and run, but they were smart; their money wasn't in plain sight, nor was it anywhere that could ever be found if the Feds raided their homes, which was definitely coming....

# CHAPTER 22

Joseph Finney walked into the F.B. I's headquarters with his taupe briefcase in hand. When he received Lexxy's call, he stopped what he was doing, making love to his sweet wife, and came straight away.

While he got dressed, he thought about what Lexxy told him, and the little bit of knowledge she seemed to have on the situation at hand. From what he could tell, the human trafficking charges wouldn't stick; that was something that was hard to prove anyway. The drugs and the murders, however, could be proven with the right evidence.

This wouldn't be his first time working on such a high-profile case, that he knew this one was turning out to be, and for that reason alone, the F.B.I. was going to receive hell. Joseph Finney made people run away from him with his witty words and his ability to find certain things out. Joseph was no stranger to the underground world. He indulged from time to time in Heroin and Cocaine, and he of course went to get the best. Dutch had been supplying him with the best Heroin and Cocaine around, but after Cocaine took back over, he became his client, and he'd been loyal to them ever since. They paid him well in drugs, so he had no problem getting out of bed to finally start repaying them for quality drugs.

When Liam saw Joseph walking up to him, his skin began trembling. He knew that Joseph was famous for getting people off, and even as confident as Liam was, seeing Joseph put a damper on his day.

"Hello, Liam," Joseph said as he approached him.

"Finney, how can I help you today?"

"Ahh….wipe that smug grin off your face. I know it's only hiding fear anyway. I'm here for my clients, the Blackwood family."

It was as Liam expected. He couldn't help but roll his eyes as he opened the door to see Paul.

Liam still hadn't even gone inside to see Quentin, Juaqeen, or even Roman just yet.

Joseph opened his briefcase as he sat down in front of Paul. Although he wasn't as familiar with him, he was still a part of their family, and just as important as any of the others.

When Paul saw his face, he couldn't have been more relieved.

"How are you doing, Paul?"

"I'd be better if I was marrying my woman instead of this shit hole. What do you know?"

"Not much just yet. I have to get some information, but the good thing is the human trafficking charges won't stick, at least not against you all. That was the kind of thing Dutch was into, but the other charges, we'll have to go against this thing head on to see how we can get you all out of this."

Paul needed to tell Joseph something, but he wasn't

sure if he was being watched, , so he grabbed some of the papers Joseph had taken out and grabbed a pen. He wrote a small note on it that said for him to give it to Cocaine.

When he read over it, he had no clue what it meant, but obviously Cocaine would.

Joseph winked at Liam and told him to be strong. He would of course do everything he could to get them out. Money was no object, so that opened up plenty of avenues for them to find a way out.

Joseph grabbed the contents of his briefcase and stuffed them back inside, only leaving out the note Paul had for Cocaine.

Liam let Joseph into the cold, dark room that held Cocaine, and he smiled.

"Joseph, took you long enough," Cocaine said as he laughed a bit.

"Yes, I was in the middle of something, but I came down as soon as I could. I just came back from seeing your brother. He asked me to give you something."

Joseph showed Cocaine the note, and it was one, single line, that read, **"The roses are dead, and the gardener killed them."**

Cocaine read the message and knew exactly what it meant. No, they were never preparing for this moment, but they knew at some point, they'd have a snake in their midst, and if that ever happened, they needed to be able to talk about it without others knowing what they were saying.

"Do you know what that means?" Joseph asked.

"I do. Can you tell me what we're looking at, Joseph?"

"Honestly, if the charges stick, twenty-five to life. The human trafficking is trash, that'll go out the window, but the rest, we'll have to work diligently to get these thrown out."

Cocaine was speechless. Shit suddenly got real. Now that he knew what they were facing, he worried that some of their secrets may not stay buried, that everything they'd ever done would be out, thrown up like vomit. Like ghosts from the past, nothing would stay hidden or buried.

Luckily, Cocaine had taught Lexxy the code, and when she saw it, she too would know what it meant, and hopefully, she would know what to do. The boys still hadn't been given phone calls, and to Cocaine's knowledge, there would be no bond, no nothing.

"Ok, so what's going to come next?"

"You'll be transported to the jail where they'll determine if you all will be given a bond. Hopefully, you will, and you'll be out in no time."

"And if not?"

"If not, then this is going to be a long ride, but you'll at least be in a place to receive visits because the girls can't see you here."

Cocaine nodded his head. The only thing he could do was hope for the best, even though all odds were against them.

This would be the first time in years he'd have to spend the night away from Lexxy, and though he wasn't a bitch, nor was he "sensitive" by any means, Lexxy was his home. Wherever she was, was where he wanted to be. He was already starting to miss his children, and his heart broke for them. He knew what it was like to grow up without a father, and he spent every day with them. This would be his first time away from them as well.

Cocaine promised himself he'd be a good father. No, an amazing father, and now, a part of his greatest accomplishment in his life was being taken away from him.

"I'm going to go over to the house to speak with Lexxy. She and the girls made it there alright. I'll do my best, I promise you, Cocaine."

Although Cocaine should've been reassured, he wasn't. He felt terrible inside. Something inside of him just knew this wasn't going to play out easy peezy, and that shit was going to go terribly before it went better.

He couldn't spend a lifetime away from his children, and he damn sure wasn't going to spend a lifetime away from his wife.

Sitting in front of Lexxy's home, the house felt like a prison, and that's what it would be without her husband, her brothers, her father-in-law…and the list went on. Just when her family was whole, it wasn't, but she felt selfish for feeling bad.

Denise's wedding day had been ruined at the hands of her own father. Lexxy placed her hand on Denise's and squeezed it lightly.

"Come on, let's go in the house."

Denise didn't speak, nor did she move. Sha sat directly across from them, feeling the same thing. Quentin was finally getting serious about her, and now, he was snatched away from her; that would definitely set their relationship back some more.

Junie and Wild Bill took the kids so Lexxy could handle her business and have some time to herself. Ella Mae said she too would go with them, hoping the children would keep her in high spirits. She couldn't believe the feds wanted an old man like Roman in prison; that just made no sense to her, and it was cruel and unusual.

"Denny, did you hear me?" Lexxy asked, calling her

best friend's nickname, hoping that would help her snap back into reality.

Denny looked at Lexxy with a tear stained face, her make up running completely off her cheeks, her eyes swollen and puffy. She didn't know what to say. Moving even just a little bit hurt, and her body and soul ached for Paul's touch. To most people, he was cold and distant, sometimes a bit mean, but with her, he was sweet, funny, and passionate, and she looked forward to a lifetime of happiness with him.

Since her father left her in the church, she'd been blowing up his phone nonstop, and being the petty man he was, he not only ignored her calls, he purposely declined them, but he was going to have to see his daughter for this. She wouldn't let this go so easily.

Sha got out of the limo first hoping it would prompt the others to follow her, but it didn't. Lexxy wasn't going to move without Denise, so Sha stood outside of the limo, reached into her purse, and pulled out a blunt. The stress of the day had become too much, and she didn't want to feel anything, and crying had worn her out. She was tired of crying, of doing nothing; something needed to be done.

"Denny, come on. I know you're hurting, but we need to go in the house. We can't sit in front of it all day. I'd rather be inside standing around it, than outside looking at it. Come on, you just gotta make it in the house."

Denise had no more energy, and she felt broken, but Lexxy was right. She did need to go in the house; they all did.

Like someone with old bones, Denise turned her

body to get out of the car, leaning on the door for support because she just knew her own legs were too wobbly to get her to the door.

Sha saw Denise's giant wedding dress hanging from the door, so she hurried up and put out her blunt and placed it back in her purse. When Denise rose from the limo, she was shaking, but Sha was there to guide her around the back to meet Lexxy on the other side.

Lexxy had gotten out the moment she saw Denise making her exit. She had to be strong not only for herself but for the entire family. Most of them looked to her for strength because of all the things she endured. Most of those things should have taken her out, but they didn't. She was stronger than ever, at least until now. It was nothing like having peace and happiness and then having it taken away from you when you least expected it.

Denise's feet felt like bricks; her shoes were off, her veil was ripped from her snatching it off her head, and her dress was dirty from crying on the ground for so long at the church, but she was going to make it in the house, even if Sha and Lexxy had to carry her in the house themselves.

Together, the three women linked arms and made their way up the stairs of the house. The limo driver felt bad for what happened to the ladies. He'd only caught a small piece of what they were saying, but it all sounded bad, and being left at a wedding any time was sad, even if the person didn't leave you.

He waited until the ladies got inside, and then he pulled off. This day started out so promising, and he loved driving for weddings; they were such joyous occasions, but this was ruined for not just them, but for him too.

When they made it inside, Sha and Lexxy helped Denise over to the couch.

"I'm gonna go get us some clothes to wear, Sha…"

"I'm already on it. What we drinkin'? Dark or light?"

"Both," Denise requested.

"Ooh, that's some dangerous shit, but I feel it."

Sha bounced off to the kitchen to make their drinks, and Lexxy returned with clothes for all of them to wear. When Lexxy looked around the house, there were pictures of Cocaine and her posted all around. She was proud to be by his side, and he felt the same way, and that could be seen no matter where you were in the house.

There was one picture in particular that stood out the most to Lexxy, and it was from their last anniversary they'd spent together. Lexxy was sick as a dog with a cold from hell, and Cocaine wound up catching the cold from her, so they spent the entire evening in bed, cuddling, watching TV, and drinking an entire bottle of Nyquil. The picture was of the two of them in bed. Lexxy had the bottle of Nyquil in one hand, tilted up to her mouth, and Cocaine was licking the side of her mouth, trying to catch any drops that might have fallen. Denise was lucky enough to catch the picture when she was coming in to bring them more soup. Sha was there being Mary

Poppins, entertaining the kids, and Denise was acting like Mrs. Doubtfire, taking care of her sick babies.

Lexxy stopped for a moment to run her fingers over the blown up picture, almost as if she could feel the memory from touching Cocaine's printed face.

Sha appeared from the kitchen with two glasses in her hands, and a bottle of wine tucked underneath her arm pit. You could always catch either a beer, some wine, or a blunt of that good-good on Sha.

She brought the glasses over to the coffee table in front of Denise, and they both took a look at Lexxy who was so lost in the memory of the sweet, unbreakable love she shared with Cocaine.

Lexxy felt her breath catching in her throat. She'd been ok until now. She promised she wouldn't cry, that Denise had done enough for the both of them and when she got alone, she'd let it rip, but she couldn't hold it in any longer.

The clothes Lexxy carried in her arms fell to the ground, and so did she. She went tumbling down the last few stairs that led into the living room.

Though she wasn't seriously hurt, or at least not physically, Sha and Denise both ran to her side and joined her on the ground.

"Let me look at you," Sha said, jumping straight into nurse mode. She still worked at the hospital. Sha was determined not to leave her job just because her man had money, and she liked helping people, so it was the perfect fit for her.

"I'm fine," Lexxy cried as she held her arm that hit the floor.

Sha got up and went back into the kitchen. She knew all too well how something small could turn into something bothersome later, so she went into the freezer to get some ice to help.

"Here, put this on it so it doesn't swell."

Lexxy placed the ice wrapped in a towel on her arm, and she hissed at the stinging feeling.

She realized now that she had to calm down, that she had to pull it together. Just as she was about to speak, there was a knock at the door.

"Who the hell could that be?" Lexxy asked as she rose from the ground to answer the door.

"Take it easy!" Sha yelled as she grabbed the clothes from the floor. "Here, go put this on. Take off your dress and pass it out to me. I'll go hang it up."

"Yeah, even though it's ruined," Denise said, defeated.

"Hush, ain't nothin' Mr. C's dry cleaner can't fix. Come on."

Sha helped Denise from the floor and they went to the hallway bathroom to get changed.

Lexxy pulled open the door, and thankfully, it was Joseph.

"Alexxus, how are you? I have something for you."

"Come in, come in."

Lexxy moved out of the way so Joseph could come in the house. He went over to the couch and gave her the message that Paul had written out. She of course recognized it and couldn't believe it was true. One of their most trusted workers had given them up. The "gardener" referred to their worker Raul who made all of their runs, did the drop offs, pick ups, and really, everything they needed done. He was a younger Wild Bill. They couldn't believe this.

"So…what are we looking at?" Sha asked as she came back into the living room along with Denise.

"As I told the boys, they're facing twenty-five years to life. Before I came over here, I made a few calls, and it seems as though there is an informant who has given up a lot of information about the boys, but they were not willing to sell out any of you. The boys will be able to have visits and phone calls as soon as tomorrow. I've already taken care of the proper paperwork necessary for emergency visits. This is going to get a lot worse before it gets better. This will definitely go to trial, and I'll be able to file a motion of discovery to see what all they have on you. There's only so much I can get, and only so much that money will pay for."

Lexxy understood that completely, and she knew who the state witness was.

"Let me ask you a question, Joseph, and this is just hypothetically speaking, if there is no one to testify, no state witness, what would happen then?" Lexxy asked, plotting.

"Hypothetically speaking, if a state witness recanted or for some reason was unable to testify, the case would be damaged and hopefully implode. That just depends on what he's already given up and the evidence they have."

"I see. Well, as always, Joseph. Thank you for your help. If you're able to speak with Cocaine before I am, please let him know that I love him."

"Us too, please," Denise murmured with her head down.

"Of course, I will. I'll be in touch."

Joseph gathered his things and left the house.

Lexxy, Denise, and Sha were now all on the couch, holding hands. A few minutes later, the three of them were drinking the drinks Sha made for them, and then, eventually, they were all drinking straight from the bottle, passing it around the room.

As the evening continued, they were so drunk, they were almost numb. Lexxy took the last sip that was in the bottle of wine and stood up.

"I—I wanna say somethin'," she said as she swayed back and forth, using the wine bottle as a microphone.

"I don't know 'bout y'all, but I won't rest until they come home. We know who the informant is, and I'll be damned if I let Raul's ass get away with this shit. I don't know what else we can do, but whatever can be done, I'm gon' do it. Now, either y'all bitches is with me, or y'all gotta get out the way."

Sha and Denise both started laughing. Lexxy was glad to see that through their drunken stupor, they were able to still laugh and find some type of humor in the situation.

"Bitch, sit yo' drunk ass down. You should already know we got yo' back. We go back like a Cadillac. Sha, you ain't been around us for that long, but we trust you, and we know you love you some Quentin, and I'll be damned if I let my stupid ass daddy take away my happiness."

Denise was on one, but she seemed more like herself in this moment than she had in the past hours.

"So then we're in this together?" Lexxy asked.

Sha and Denise nodded their heads in agreement. Of course they were with it. They would do anything to get their men back, even if it meant kill. Lexxy only had the one body, but if she had to kill family members at this point to get her man out of trouble and keep the rest of her family safe, she would.

That night, the three of them made a pact to do whatever needed to be done in order to save their family. Sha was new to this dynamic, but she was a rider. She fell in love with Quentin the first time she saw him, and she wasn't going to let go of him for anything in this world.

The next day when Lexxy woke up, she looked around her living room, and it was completely trashed. She didn't even remember falling asleep. Here she was thirty years old, partying like a teenager, but it felt good to release some of the steam and sadness she felt.

She looked around the room, and Denise and Sha were cuddled up on the couch together like twins. It was cute, and they seemed to be sleeping peacefully, so Lexxy didn't want to wake them up with her loud stomping that she was known for.

Her phone was in the chair across the room, so she teetered around the room, going toward the chair. When she picked it up and saw the time, she realized they'd overslept. Joseph text Lexxy the night before and told her they had a scheduled visit for ten a.m. At the time when she saw the message, she thought for sure she wouldn't be drunk enough to forget or miss it, but she was now four hours late, and she knew there was no way they were going to get in at this time.

Lexxy plopped down in the chair going through her text messages. There were a few from her mother and father, asking her to call when she got a chance so they could check on her. There were pictures of the twins terrorizing Ella Mae, destroying the house. Lexxy was so happy that even in a time of destruction, her babies were ok, and they were feeling happy.

There were two voicemails at the top of her phone, so she pulled her screen down and clicked on the first one that was from a number she didn't recognize.

"Hey, my Sexy Lexxy. I ain't even trippin' that you missed the visit. I hope you sleepin' good and remembered to eat. Where my kids at though? Kiss them and tell 'em daddy loves and misses them, and daddy loves and misses you too. Keep your head up, mama. You too strong to let this beat you down, and I swear we been through worse. We can get through anything as long as we stick together. Shit, they got a nigga over here in the county feelin' like a king. Niggas 'round her offerin' us shit. I thought for sure they was gon' separate us, but I know Joseph helped with that. Pops and g-daddy in here actin' all old and shit, playin' cards, but look, I gotta go. I'ma call you later. Put some money on the phone. Call Globaltell Link just buy a phone card, then put some money on a nigga's books, baby, so I can order some commissary. I love you, Mrs. Blackwood. I'ma call you around three, so you better answer."

Lexxy pressed the phone to her heart; it was as if Cocaine's words were still playing in her mind and transcending to her sould. As she was smiling basking in Cocaine's love from far away, she felt like there were eyes on her, and when she looked up, Sha and Denise were smiling like little girls at her.

"So, the boys are ok?" Sha asked as she jumped up from the couch, stretching her arms out.

Denise's hair that had been in a pony tail was now covering her face and matted in the back.

Denise lifted her head from the couch and instantly regret it. She placed her hand behind her head to feel the pulsating beat of her drunken brain.

"Mmm…let me just lay back down. Go ahead with whatever you're saying, but say it quietly. My body hurts."

"I hadn't really said anything yet, but the boys are ok, at least it seems like it. But get y'all asses up. We need to put some money on the phones. Cocaine said he was calling around three, so Paul and Quentin could be calling before or after, but I don't even know where my damn wallet is."

Sha wobbled over to her purse and poured out its contents. She'd been the person to keep up with everything at the wedding when shit started popping off. She knew at some point, they'd all need their personal belongings, so she scooped them up and put them in her purse, now she was glad she did that.

They each grabbed their wallets and their phones and called the number that Lexxy googled for them to put money on their phones, and afterwards, they got online and put money on their books so they could order whatever they wanted. Lexxy knew Cocaine was going to eat up everything, so he needed a lot of money on his account.

After getting the boys set up, Sha and Denise looked at one another and already knew what time it was. "We need to go home and change our clothes. We smell like alcohol and ass, and the two of those together nor separately match. Come on Sha-Sha, let's go," Denise said as she began walking toward the door.

"I'll go with you. I don't really want to be alone right now."

Denise felt like an idiot for not inviting her best friend to go along with them.

"Of course you don't. Come on. I don't know how we thought we were going to get there anyway. The cars are still at the church. I don't even want to think about yesterday. Let's just go change our clothes, and we can worry about the rest later."

"Agreed," Lexxy and Sha said at the same time.

Lexxy grabbed her keys, slid on her house shoes and kicked Sha and Denise a pair, and headed to the car.

When they got to Paul and Quentin's, which was also Denise and Sha's home as well, they went straight in and got to showering. Lexxy, who still had on her clothes from the day before, sat at the bar after pouring herself a drink.

Sha and Denise were in separate bathrooms, causing a lot of noise during their showers. They were acting as if they were four-hundred-pound sumo wrestlers they were stomping around upstairs, but even in all of that noise, there was a noise Lexxy couldn't miss.

It sounded as if a beeping sound was coming from the wall, which of course, in any house, would be strange, unless it was a phone, but the last time Lexxy heard anything beep like that was in the nineties, the first time she heard the sound of a beeper.

Lexxy followed the sound, and at first, she thought it was coming from the wall, but the closer she got to it, she realized it came from the bookshelf that was tilted against the wall.

She began looking at the books, studying them, wondering where this was going, then she started pulling books on the shelf, in an effort to stop the sound and find out what the hell it was.

Book after book she tossed to the ground, and finally, after she was surrounded in books and only three remained, the beeping sound was closer than it had been the entire time. She was close. She opened another book, flipping through its pages, and then she found it. Inside was a tape recorder with a red button on it.

Lexxy didn't want to flip out because the tape recorder was still recording, and she didn't want to stop the recording because she didn't know who was listening on the other end, but she needed to let Sha and Denise know so they didn't say anything incriminating.

Carefully, Lexxy walked up the stairs and opened the bathroom door to where Sha was butt, booty hole naked. Sha was about to squeal when she saw Lexxy, but she quickly put her finger to her mouth, telling her to be quiet.

Sha's eyebrows furrowed, and Lexxy showed her the tape recorder.

Sha's arms went up in confusion. Lexxy motioned her arms for her to follow her so she could show Denise.

Denise had the other bathroom door open, so she went inside and showed her the tape recorder.

Denise had seen once on Law & Order where you could interrupt the recording by making more noise, so Denise cut the shower back on with both nobs, and they closed the bathroom door so it would be too loud for anything they might say on the recorder.

Still whispering, Denise asked, "What the fuck? Where did you get that?"

"Downstairs in the bookcase. I kept hearing something beeping, and I had to figure out what it was because it was driving me crazy, and this is what came out of one of the books. We need to know what's on the other end, but if we stop the recording, whoever is listening on the other side will know we've got it."

Sha took the tape recorder and left the bathroom. Both Denise and Lexxy were confused by what she was going to do.

"Fuck it. I say we play it. Whoever left it here had to know this was something that could have been found, so fuck it."

Sha stopped recording and hit the play button.

As the girls stood in the hallway, the tape recorder went on for hours, and on it was all types of incriminating stuff. Lexxy already knew who the snitch was, but she couldn't figure out why he would do something like this.

The family often joked about Dutch's death; it was funny to them, and also, it was what set their family free. Quentin and Paul had brought up the fact that Lexxy killed Carley, and there were recordings of their drug operations and so much more.

"We're screwed," Lexxy said.

"No, no, not necessarily. They went after the boys, but not us. They want them, not us, because you bold faced killed Carley, and they haven't come after you yet." Sha was positive that if they were wanted for something, they'd be in lock up just like the boys.

"Y'all hurry up and get dressed, we got some moves to make. Y'all meet me outside. I'm 'bout to make a phone call."

Lexxy stepped outside and got back into her car. She couldn't believe after all they did for Raul and his family that he would be so easily persuaded to rat on them. The recording even told about their clean up crew and where they dumped the bodies. This wasn't good.

Lexxy pulled out her phone and called Joseph. She needed to know what could be done about this.

"Hello? Alexxus, I was just about to call you. I need to warn you."

"Warn me about what?" Lexxy asked, wondering what the fuck could be next.

"The feds are planning on raiding the houses, the trap spots, everything."

"Oh God, when?"

"Today. I don't know when, but sometime today. Luckily, you and the girls don't have taps on your phones, but I would ditch them anyway. Get as much stuff out as you possibly can before they come. My fed friend said it will be happening sometime today, but he's unsure of the time."

"Ok, thanks, Joseph, but listen, one more thing, I found a tape

Lexxy ended the call and ran back in the house. She checked the tape recorder to make sure that it wasn't recording, and then she began yelling.

"Get everything you can. Use the boy's cars or whatever you gotta do. The feds are planning a raid for some time today. I don't want to split up, but we have to. Meet me at my mama and daddy's house later on. I'll be waiting for you there."

Denise and Sha stood at the top of the stairs not believing what was going on around them. Their lives had been tossed and turned in the worst way, and this shit right here was about to take them out of the race.

Lexxy raced back to her house, and when she got inside, she moved like the Flash; the only thing she was missing was the lightning coming off of her. She went into the kids' room and opened up the backs of their teddies where some of the money was stashed. She had several large bags with her, and once she filled one up, she threw it down the stairs. She wouldn't have time to be carrying those heavy ass bags down the stairs.

She went from room to room, clearing out the money they had, stuffing it into the bags. The money inside the house was easy to get; it would be the money outside she'd have to use a little elbow grease for.

After putting the first couple of bags she had in the car, she went out back and dug like she was a slave on the Underground Railroad, digging her way to freedom. When she finally reached the four large garbage bags, she pulled them out, sweat dripping into her eyes. She then ran over to the pre-plotted plants they bought and shoved them into the ground, to make it seem as though this was just a regular gardening project in case they did come back and look. She covered it with dirt and ran back into the house. She had one more spot to get to before she could actually leave. Underneath their couch was a floor safe, where Cocaine had kept the bricks and the letter his mother had written to him before he was born. If she could get nothing else, she would make sure she got this. The money was nice to have, and they were more than likely going to need it, but these bricks were sentimental, they were a part of who Cocaine was.

Lexxy pushed the couch over, and underneath was a magnet. This magnet was the only thing that would lift the weight inside of the safe once the code was inside. The code was long as hell, on purpose, for just in case if someone was trying to get inside. Lexxy thought about the tape recorder she found in Paul and Quentin's, and she wondered if Raul had bugged her place as well, but he couldn't have. They never allowed him in the house, and Paul and Quentin had more to do with the day to day operations than Cocaine did, but she didn't have time to search either way.

She unlocked the safe using the ten-digit code, and

then, she used the magnet to pull the weight up. The weight and magnet were designed by a colleague of hers at the hospital. He was a scientist who spent a lot of time around the hospital. When his home was broken in, he then designed this magnet specific weight to keep people from getting inside of his home, and it worked, so Lexxy bought one for her and Cocaine, just one, to see how it would work, and so far, it had worked perfectly. It was also supposed to be undetectable. Without the weight, an alarm would go off, signaling somebody was trying to get your shit.

Lexxy pulled the weight up, got the bricks, and she fled the house. She knew she could return later when the Feds were gone; she just hoped she'd make it out ok. As she was coming outside, she saw lights coming toward the driveway.

Quickly, she got in her car, started it up, and pulled off to the back. She could still get out through the back, and hopefully, no one would even know she was gone.

An hour later, Lexxy arrived at her parents' house, and Sha and Denise weren't too far behind her. Wild Bill ran out, trying to help them unload their things into the house.

"Hey, baby girl, how you holdin' up?" he asked as he held Lexxy tightly.

"I'm ok, Daddy. Right now, I just wanna get this stuff out of plain sight, you know?"

"I do. Come on."

One by one, they unloaded their cars, and Wild Bill took everything down to their basement. Lexxy remembered to bring the weight and the magnet, and no matter what, she hoped, the feds wouldn't dare come to this house, but if they did, they'd have a hard time getting anything out of this house.

Once everything was unloaded and tucked safely, Lexxy began thinking about the house they murdered Dutch in. Thank God Wild Bill sold the house shortly after, and he'd bought it under an alias anyway, so he would be safe, or at least she hoped.

Lexxy sat down on the couch, and Sha and Denise were in the kitchen with Junie and Ella Mae, and suddenly, Lexxy heard footsteps pattering toward her. She would know those Fred Flinstone feet anywhere, they got it from her.

"Mommy!" Alexiana and CJ yelled as they attacked her with hugs and kisses.

"Hi, babies. Mmm…Mama missed you so, so much."

As Lexxy held on to her children, kissing their tiny heads and faces, she wondered how she was going to get the boys out of this and what she was going to do. She loved her children, and she loved Cocaine, but what if this blew up in all of their faces and she had an opportunity to save them?

Running wasn't her style, but if she had to, she would. She would do anything for her children, and she knew Cocaine would want her to do the same, even if it meant leaving him behind.

For the moment, they were safe, but how long would that last?

Lexxy stared at her family, memories flooding her brain, and she knew she had to put a plan in motion, to boss up harder than when she killed Carley. She was about to have to hold Cocaine down and lift him back up, but when all of this was said and done, their enemies would be laid to waste, and finally, they would live out their lives, and go the fuck on!

Denise had waited long enough for her father to return her calls, and after going home the next morning and finding their house in disarray from the feds raiding the place, she knew she had to go and see her father. She tried to give him a chance to come clean, to admit to his wrong doings, but he didn't. He was hiding from her like a coward, and that wasn't like him, which let her know he would be afraid of her response to all of this. But what did he expect? That she was going to be ok with how all of this went down? She needed answers, today.

When Denise arrived at her father's house, his car was parked right outside, so she knew he was home. She didn't even bother knocking because she had a key. It had been a very long time since she'd been in her family home, but now, she was coming to get some type of understanding of what the fuck her father thought he was doing when he not only ruined her wedding day, but her life.

The door opened creakily; Liam still hadn't gotten that door fixed. It had always been noisy, since they first moved in. She shook her head, and came straight in. Instead of addressing her father as such, she addressed him as if he were a stranger, someone who didn't raise her.

"Liam! Liam, we need to talk!"

Denise threw her purse and keys on the couch and waited for him to meet her downstairs. She knew he was probably in his office, his man cave, possibly doing some more plotting.

When he didn't come out, she marched straight to the back and went into his office.

"Liam, I know you heard me calling you."

"I'm sorry, I don't respond to children who have clearly forgotten that I'm still their father."

"I'm not a child."

"No, but you're MY child, Denise, and you will respect me."

"Oh, the way you respected me, right? The way you respected me when you ruined my wedding, the way you respected me by lying to me, the way you respected me when you had the feds toss my home, and now it looks like a war zone. Respect my ass!"

Denise was furious. Fire literally seemed like it was blowing out of her ears.

"Denise, I don't know what you've come here to accomplish. If it's to scream at me, scream your bratty head off, otherwise, I have shit to do, and I'm not even going to stand in here and listen to you do that."

Liam was so upset, he just left the room, not even realizing what he'd left on his desk. Through her peripheral vision, Denise was able to see something Liam left on his desk. On the side of the manila envelope was a name written in bold letters: **Leon Jessup.**

Denise knew she couldn't take the whole file; she wouldn't be able to sneak it out of there without her father knowing, so she snatched the file open and retrieved her phone from her pocket and began taking pictures, trying to get through it as quickly as possible without her father knowing. From the door, she kept looking around the corner to see if he was coming, while still trying to get good angles of the pictures she was taking. The file was thick, and it had a lot of information, but she hoped she could get it all.

Liam started yelling again, and the closer his voice got, her heart rate went up. Though Liam was her father, this was a man she didn't know. She had no idea what he was capable of at this point. Liam was no longer the man she considered her father; they'd fallen out years ago anyway when she didn't want to go directly to college.

After being in high school for four years straight, Denise wanted a little freedom, so instead of going straight to school, she went and got a job to support herself because she didn't want to take money from her father. She thought he had a security company, which he did, but it was just a front, but when she thought that, she didn't want to take money out of her father's pocket. Her working would help out in the house with the bills, though he didn't need any help, but Denise was an independent person, even as a teenager, and her father hated that she could think on her own and didn't need someone making decisions for her. She wasn't easily manipulated, at least not as she got older, and because of that, Liam told her if she wanted to throw her life away and ruin the life he'd set up for her, then she could; she just couldn't do it in his house, and that created tension and a rift in their relationship. Since then, it's been a power struggle between the two, which ultimately led to her not inviting Liam to the wedding, or even really letting him know how serious she was with Paul, but now she knew that he knew way more than he was letting on.

"And another thing, you think you so grown, that you can just do whatever you wanna do and say whatever you want, get the fuck out of my house, Denise. I had hoped that we could reconcile whatever differences we had between us."

"You didn't want to reconcile; you wanted me to behave, to be obedient like a dog would. I'm not an animal—you can't command me!"

Thankfully, Denise had been able to close the file and put it back in its proper place just in time before Liam could rush in to complain some more, and now that he was back in there, she didn't want to listen to another word of what he had to say. If he wasn't going to apologize for what he did, or give up some information, there was no reason for her to be there, but she wasn't leaving empty handed.

Denise left her father's office and went back into the front room to grab her keys and purse. When she reached for the door, Liam grabbed her wrist and said, "This could have been much easier, so much simpler if you weren't always acting out. You fell for the wrong guy, got into the wrong crowd, and now, you're going to have to suffer the loss of those consequences."

Denise looked at Liam's hand around her wrist and snatched away from his grip.

"And now you'll have to mourn the loss of your only daughter. This is your last chance, Liam. You have the power to fix all of this, the question is, will you? Will you fix this so you don't lose your child?"

She took a long, deep look into Liam's eyes and quickly realized when he didn't answer, that he wouldn't be of any help.

"That's what I thought."

Denise opened the door and slammed it behind her. She wished she had tears to cry over this situation, but she was all cried out when it came to her father, and there was nothing left for her to get out of her system. This was what she expected, completely. It was times like this where she wished she had a mother to confide in. Often times, whenever she felt down, she went to Junie because she was there for Denise as a teenager. She was the one who told her about sex and how to protect herself. When she got her first heartbreak, Junie stayed up with her all night, rocking her back and forth like a mother should. Her mother was nowhere to be found, and this late in the game, she didn't know if she even wanted to find her.

If a mother could leave their daughter, she was probably trash, but then there was always that part of Denise that wondered if it was her father who ran her mother away. There were plenty of times when she wished she had an escape, so she could only imagine how her mother might have felt.

Either way, that was something that she would never know.

When Denise got into her car, she went and pulled

up the pictures that she'd taken on her phone. There was a feeling that was eating at her in the pit of her stomach, and she had to know what it was. What happened?

As she scanned the photos, it told about who Leon was—a caretaker to the Blackwood family, and he died not long ago, and when she continued reading over everything, there was one thing that stuck out to her the most.

Dutch Hassle=murderer.

If Dutch killed Leon, why would Liam be protecting that? Why was he trying to bring the Blackwood men up on some false charges? There was a skunk in the air, and something stank, and Denise was on her way to finding it. She just hoped it wouldn't be too late to save the boys with this new information.

Standing over what should have been Jayla's grave, Leon rubbed the headstone Roman paid for. He wished she was still here, that she could see Cocaine as a grown man. He was the man that Juaqeen would have wanted him to be, minus his thirst for vengeance.

Cocaine had been gone for some time now, and Leon hadn't heard from him. All he could do was hope that he was ok and that wherever he was, he was happy with his life.

Leon turned around, ready to leave the gravesite and go back home, when he was stopped by a man he'd seen only a handful of times before, and the man who shot Juaqeen.

Leon began taking a few steps backwards, trying to get away from him. He didn't know why after all these years, he'd still be hanging around, and even more so, why he'd be here at the cemetery was beyond Leon's thought process.

"Mmm…Leon, you're going to make this moment even sweeter."

"What moment?" Leon asked, fear quivering in his throat.

"Well, I came to get Jayla's body, I need to work something out with Cocaine, and this is the only way."

Leon had to think quickly. He wasn't going to let Dutch just take Jayla like this. He stood in front of the grave and said, "I won't let you do this, Dutch. Whatever you're thinking, try *something else. What do you mean work something out with him? You know where he is?"*

"Of course I do. He's here, in Texas, come to see his grandmother I suppose. But that's neither here nor there. Sad, isn't it? He came all the way here and had nothing to say to you? Terrible, now if you'll move aside."

"No! I won't be moving aside. I'm not gonna let you do this!"

Leon did the only thing he could think to do—he yelled, hoping someone would hear him and someone would come over and help him, to stop Dutch, but Dutch had already paid off the owner and the caretaker; there would be no one coming to his rescue.

"Help! Help!"

Dutch pulled out his gun and knocked him out with the butt of it. Leon reached for his head and then fell to the ground. Dutch's henchmen approached the grave and started shoveling their way into it. Leon was in so much pain, that when the henchmen were digging the grave up, he could barely see what was going on, but then, he remembered he had his phone.

Checking to make sure no one was paying him any attention, he slowly pulled his phone out and began dialing Roman's number to warn him, but it was too late. Before he could even press the send button, Dutch shot him in the head.

Leon was a good man, and he didn't deserve to die like a dog. After shooting him, Dutch didn't even have the decency to bury him or even have him moved. He told the cemetery staff to deal with it, and they did. They buried him in an unmarked grave. Dutch paid them to do so, so that their beloved Leon would never be found again, but nothing ever truly dies, even if it only disappears for some time.

Jonah, who had given the truth to Roman didn't think that the two incidents were related. He instead informed the local police, and of course, as a federal agent, Liam was all over that. Anything connecting him to the Blackwood family was right up his alley.

Shortly after, Dutch turned up dead. He wasn't the one Liam truly wanted, not anymore, he was after the bigger fish like Juaqeen, Cocaine, and Roman. Dutch was just the one who started it all.

So, it was easier for him to frame the boys, that they somehow had something to do with the murder than Dutch, a dead man, who would be overlooked.

Liam was tired of justice being escaped, and this time, he promised himself, that he would get the justice all of his victims deserved, even the future victims that he wouldn't be able to later save…

ONE WEEK LATER....

After Denise showed the girls the pictures in her phone, they gave the pictures along with the tape recorder to Joseph and let him start digging.

Since they missed their first visit with the boys, they had to wait until the following week, and even though they missed them, they dreaded seeing them like that. They were used to their men being on the outside, enjoying life with them, not held captive in a state dungeon.

From what they understood, although the girls were against it, Joseph said going to trial may be their best bet at winning at something like this. There was some evidence that would be inadmissible, thus ridding them of certain charges, or at least take the amount of years they could potentially serve down.

Before they went to the jail, Joseph prepped them on the appropriate clothes they could wear while visiting, and since only Cocaine and Lexxy were married, they'd be the only ones allowed to see one another face to face. Unfortunately, Denise and Sha would only be able to see

Paul and Quentin through a thick piece of glass, and only hear each other through a dirty ass wall pay phone.

As they stood outside, waiting to go in, they joined hands and looked at one another. This situation had gotten ugly fast, and they didn't know if they'd be able to get out of this one. It seemed like it would be easy to, but now, even with all the money in the world, it wasn't that easy, and they were still trying to put the pieces together, but there were so many things missing, like where was Raul? He was normally one of the easiest people in the world to find, but now, of course, he was running from them, so he had gotten ghost, and he left no trace, not of him or his family.

How could Liam want the boys so bad, he was willing to frame them for a murder they didn't commit? That just didn't make sense, and even though Lexxy was the one who killed Carley, Cocaine told her to keep her mouth shut about it, that if the feds didn't know it was her, there was no need for them to know now, but Lexxy was uncomfortable with that. It wasn't that she enjoyed gloating about the way she took Carley's traitorous, crazy ass out, but she didn't want the boys to get anything else added on to their sentence for something she did and would admit to doing.

Taking deep breaths, Denise, Lexxy, and Sha walked in with their heads held high, supporting one another, the way it was supposed to be. One by one, they went up to the visitor's window and signed in and waited to be escorted to their proper meeting areas.

Lexxy was the first to go back, and she couldn't wait to see her man. She was thrilled on the inside because even though it had only been a little over a week since she last saw him, going a day without his touch felt like a lifetime.

When she came into the room, Cocaine was sitting at the table with a giant smile on his face. He couldn't wait to see his woman. She ran straight over to the table trying to kiss him, and the guard stopped her.

"No kissing allowed, ma'am."

Lexxy looked at him with a confused face, and Cocaine just laughed. "Sit down, baby."

Lexxy sat down at the table and immediately reached for his hand. After a thorough search of her belongings, they finally let her back there to see her man.

"Baby, how are you? Are you ok?" Lexxy asked as she looked as far as she could see. She even looked under the table to see what on him she could see to make sure he was ok.

"I'm fine, Sexy Lexxy. How are you, baby? How you holdin' up?"

"I don't wanna talk about me. I wanna talk about you. I love you so much, Coco. This has been the hardest week ever."

"I know, beautiful, but you gotta be strong, ok?"

"I'm trying. I really am. How's your dad, Roman?"

"They're good. They in here bein' the old niggas they are. Everything is cool, baby. Don't worry about us. We've seen worse, I promise. The worst part is not being able to hold you at night or at all."

Lexxy squeezed his hand; she felt the same way.

"How are the kids? They cool?"

"They're fine. They ask for you every night. Alexiana

sleeps with one of your shirts, and CJ is trying to be strong. He's just like you."

Hearing about his children made his eyes water. He was trying to be strong, but the truth was he was struggling every day to keep a cool head, but he couldn't tell Lexxy that, or she would lose it. She would lose the small piece of sanity she was holding on to.

"How are Quentin and Paul? They ok?"

Cocaine shook his head. Paul was being tough; he always had been, but Quentin, he was sweating bullets, losing his mind. He would never snitch, he would never give up the family secrets, but being in jail was affecting him more than he was willing to admit out loud.

"Paul is Paul, you know how that nigga is, but Quentin, I don't know, baby. I don't know how Q really is doing. I think seeing Sha might help him; I'm hoping it helps."

Cocaine and Lexxy sat talking for the next hour about what they would do when Cocaine got out. Lexxy, in between the guards' stares, was showing Cocaine her breasts, the only thing she could whip out. She wanted him to know she was still wanting him. His dick was hard at just seeing her cleavage. He was used to being able to fuck her anytime, and now, this shit was killing him. He missed dipping into his wife when he felt like it.

Over and over again, Cocaine told Lexxy how much he loved her and how he was going to fuck her the moment he could. She didn't know it, but Cocaine had written her a letter for every day he was inside, and now that he had his commissary, he was going to send the letters out.

He hoped he didn't have to do a lot of time, but if he did, Lexxy would never forget how much he loved her and how much he thought about her. In truth, Lexxy was the only thing that kept his mind together—her and the kids.

Sha and Denise sat at the small phone booths waiting for Quentin and Paul to come and meet them on the other side of the glass. They both promised each other they wouldn't cry, but that wasn't something they could guarantee realistically. Denise already had tears in her eyes, and Sha, her heart broke the moment Quentin was taken from her. She was barely making it from one minute to the next.

When Quentin and Paul finally sat down at the chairs, they were all in shambles. Denise was standing up with one hand on the glass and another on the phone. Paul picked up the phone, and as soon as they confirmed that they could hear one another, Paul said, "I love you, baby. I love you so much," as he put his head up against the glass.

"I love you, too, Paul. Did Joseph tell you what we found at the house?"

"Yeah, a tape recorder. That shit is crazy. We ain't have no clue that that was in the house. Just goes to show even the niggas you grow up with, you can't always trust 'em, but Joseph is pretty optimistic that this will work out in our favor. They're gonna try and play the disgruntled worker approach, coercion type shit."

Denise just nodded her head. Most of this she already knew, but it was nice to know that Paul was kept in the loop.

"Baby, I got a favor to ask of you, and you might say no, but I'ma ask it anyway."

"Anything, daddy, anything you say. What is it?"

"I need you to try and play nice with your pops. You ain't never gon' get another chance to get some information out of him, so you need to let that shit go. No matter what happens to me, I want you to make up with him. I ain't even trippin'; this is the life I chose. Eventually, something was going to happen, and your pops was just doing his job. Now, why he was trying to throw Leon's murder on them was beyond him, but still, he loved Denise, and he knew what it was like to be at unrest with a father. He never thought he had a problem with his father while he was alive, but once he died, there were things that kept coming up more and more, especially the whole Jayla situation. He'd never get the chance to confront his father, he'd never have the opportunity to hear his side of things, and that ate him up. He didn't want that unresolved life for Denise. There was just no way something like that was going to happen.

"I would do anything you ask of me, but that, I don't know, Paul. Look at what he's done. He took you away from me, and I don't know if I'll ever be able to forgive him for this."

"Forgive him for you, not for him, baby. This life ain't promised to none of us, and with snakes in the grass, the house, and the car, we don't know what might happen, and I don't want this to be something you later regret just because of me. I'm telling you to let it go."

Denise didn't know if she could do what Paul was asking of her, but she said she would try because she loved him, and if this was his only request of her, she would do her best to make it so.

Quentin sat in front of Sha, distantly, barely looking at her.

"Q, talk to me, baby. What's wrong?"

"What's not wrong? I'm in here, and I can't even take care of you from this fuckin' hell. I can't do nothin' for you here. I can't be with you, I can't take care of you, I can't do shit for you here, Sha. If you was smart, you'd go on about your business and find somebody else."

Sha couldn't believe what she was hearing. After all the hard work she'd put into their relationship, after she stayed around when a smart person would have already left, there was no way she was going to let Quentin dictate to her what she should or should not be doing. No fucking way!

"Quentin, I love you, so excuse me for what I'm about to say, but you done lost your rabbit ass mind if you think you can push me away so fucking easily. After all these years, and you finally see me for what I'm worth, and you know that I'm gon' hold you down, nigga, you'd be a fool to try and cut me loose, and I ain't goin' nowhere no matter what you gotta say, so shut your menstrual cycle having ass the fuck up and listen to me. I love you with every breath in my fucking body, and I ain't goin' nowhere. You can try to push me away as much as you want to, but I'm not….fucking…leaving. You got me? Now tell me you love me. I ain't got all day!"

Sha kicked back in her chair and waited for him to respond. He wasn't expecting her to react this way, and shit, maybe they were both crazy. The definition of insanity is doing the same thing expecting different results. They'd been going around and around in circles for most of their relationship, and now that they were finally settled, if Quentin thought he was going to be able to get rid of Sha that easily, he was clearly fucked up in the mind.

He was speechless. He didn't really know what to say. All he could do was shake his head and laugh a bit. This was the first time he'd smiled in days. Sure, it was nice to have his brothers and Juaqeen locked up with him, but it was nothing like being away from Sha. She made him laugh, and she made him a better person. Without her, he was sure to lose his mind, one way or another.

"I'm sorry, baby. Forgive me? I'm just goin' crazy in this muthafucka."

"I get it. I'm goin' crazy without you too, daddy, but we gon' be ok. We'll figure out a way to make this work. We both just gotta be strong, and I'ma write you every chance I get."

"I don't want letters, baby. I got money on the phone so I can hear that sexy ass voice. What I want is to see some pictures of my woman so I can spill a couple of kids into some socks or a toilet or sumn'. You got me?"

Sha giggled. She loved when Quentin talked dirty to her. She stood up from her chair and turned around, revealing her ass to him. Since she'd been fucking around with Quentin, she was getting super thick, and she looked damn good.

Quentin's mouth almost started watering, he was damn near drooling.

"You lookin' good for daddy as always."

"Only for you, baby. I'ma see how risqué the pictures can be, and I'll send you whatever I can so you can let off a few kids, but don't let go of too many. When you come home, I'm havin' your baby."

"Woah, woah, I don't know about that, baby."

"Shut up, Quentin. When you see how far I'm willin' to ride for you, you won't have no choice but to wife me and slide some babies in my uterus."

"Yeah, ok, Sha-Sha."

Their visits were wonderful, and even though they were all missing one another, laying eyes directly on their men was the best thing for them at this time. It kind of helped to soothe the parts that felt broken inside of them.

Lexxy, Denise, and Sha all met back up at the car. The three of them were all happy that Junie, Ella Mae, and even Jayla had come without them because they were all trying to be strong for one another, that they didn't know if they'd just break down in front of them. Jayla had gone to stay with Junie and Wild Bill. Staying in her home without Juaqeen was turning out to not only be uncomfortable, but it made her miserable, and she didn't want to be there without him.

But Jayla was used to being without Juaqeen. She'd spent many years thinking he was dead. The only difference between now and then is the fact that she could still hear his voice, touch him, and see him, but it was almost like when they were dating. She had to wait for him to call her, for him to show up for her. She could never reach him when she needed to. It hurt then, and it hurt now, but she was one of the toughest of the Blackwood women, and she knew how to hold her man down.

As they were getting in the car, Lexxy's stomach began to feel weak, as if something inside of her was trying to come out, and sure enough, before she could even slide in the car, she was doubled over, throwing her guts up on the sidewalk.

Sha and Denise ran to her side. Denise held her hair back, and Sha soothingly rubbed her back.

"I know, girl, it fucked with us, too. You ok?" Denise asked as she continued to try and provide comfort.

"Oh, God, not again," Lexxy whispered. She remembered the last time she felt like this, she was pregnant with the twins.

"Not again, what?" Sha was clueless.

"I think I'm pregnant, again."

Sha and Denise both rose to an upright position and looked at Lexxy. This couldn't have come at a worse time, but neither of them would dare say anything like that.

"Come on, let's get you home. I'll drive," Denise suggested.

They helped Lexxy in the car, and Denise got behind the driver's seat, and as she did, she felt her phone start buzzing. She looked at it, and it was a text from Joseph.

"The trial starts December 3rd. I'll start prepping you all right away, and keep you abreast of the situation."

Denise text back a simple ok, but her thoughts kept going back to Lexxy. Depending on how far along she was, she would practically be about to have her baby around the trial time, and she knew Cocaine would not handle this well, not at all.

FIVE MONTHS LATER...

Against their better judgement, Denise, Lexxy, and Sha stopped looking for Raul. Joseph told them that if they did something to him before the trial, it would be obvious that it was them, and then they'd all be in jail. Now if something were to happen to him before they would've decided they were going to trial, then that could have been anyone, but by now, the feds knew they had plenty of time to find him, and they knew that the tape recorder had been moved, but they were prepared for their defense.

Liam had been waiting for this moment for far too long to let them slip through his fingertips.

Lexxy had been steering clear of Cocaine the last month, since she started showing. Before, it was ok because she just looked like she was putting on weight, and he mentioned it a few times before, saying little things like, "Damn baby, you been eatin' good," or "Lexxy, you gettin' thick on me, big baby?" She thought it was cute, but she knew he wouldn't be thrilled about them having a baby right now while his life hung in the balance. Even though she was excited and couldn't wait to drop this load, she also felt dead inside because she couldn't share this moment with her husband. She'd been keeping it a secret from everyone. The only people who knew were Denise and Sha, and she'd sworn them to secrecy. She'd even been wearing extra or larger clothing to keep the secret. Right now, her family needed her to be on the up and up, and if they had to worry about her and a pregnancy, they would all lose focus.

The trial had begun, and Lexxy was in court every day, sitting in the court room before Cocaine so she could get adjusted in her seat without him seeing her growing belly. For five months straight, they were denied bail; clearly, they wanted to see all of them hang.

Every day, there was a new factoid or a new piece of evidence, condemning the Blackwood men. Though Leon's murder was thrown out, it was brought up time and time again, and Cocaine wished he would have thought to stop by and see Leon before he left Texas, but he couldn't have known that he would never see him again, but life was short, and it wasn't promised to any of them, which was sadder than ever.

Every time Cocaine saw Lexxy's face in that courtroom, it lifted his spirits. Even though it was looking like they were going to be put away for a very long time, that didn't stop him from feeling how he felt. Each day, the Blackwood women came to support their men, and they stayed, no matter what it looked like. Some days were better than others, but most of the days were terrible, and each day, it seemed to look worse and worse for their fates.

On the final day of the trial, judgement day, no

matter what, Lexxy wasn't leaving until she got to hug and kiss her man, period. Joseph told them about the odds and how they may not be in their favor. It seemed as though the jury was leaning toward a guilty verdict, and they would be right. The human trafficking charges were dropped, and so were the charges for Leon's murder, but there was still Dutch's murder, Carley's murder, and all the drugs. There was no getting away from that.

The jury had been deliberating for days, going back and forth over the evidence. This was the toughest call they'd ever had to make, but today, they had no choice; they had to put an end to this.

"All rise! The honorable Judge Givens presiding over the state vs. Juaqeen, Paul, Quentin, Roman, and Cocaine Blackwood."

"You may be seated," Judge Givens said as he took a seat in his swiveled chair. Lexxy, Denise, and Sha had been sitting in the court room for over three hours, waiting, trying to get their nerves down. The more they sat at home, the crazier they were starting to feel. When the men came into the courtroom, each of them gasped, taking in their beings, knowing this may be the last time they'd see them this way for a very long time.

Judge Givens was one of the toughest judges in Nashville. He was known for locking folks up, giving them the maximum sentence possible, but he wasn't above bribery. Joseph offered him twenty-five-thousand dollars to give them a lesser sentence, and he'd taken the money.

There was no way they weren't going to jail, but at

least they wouldn't have to spend the rest of their lives in a cell, away from their family.

Getting right into it, Judge Givens asked the jury for their verdicts. Closing statements and arguments had already been given, so there was nothing left to say other than how guilty they were. Judge Givens read the sentencing each charge could carry, and everyone in the courtroom held their breath. If it wasn't for the realization that they were all alive, someone on the outside would've thought they were all wax statues they were sitting so still.

"How do you find the defendants?"

One of the women in the jury section stood from her seat, pushed her glasses back against her face, and she cleared her throat.

"In the murder of Carley Boden, we find the defendants innocent."

Lexxy wasn't surprised. She was the one who killed Carley, not the boys, and the feds knew that. That wasn't what they really wanted them for anyway. The Blackwood family supplied everybody with drugs—the streets, corporate America, the list was never ending, but this was a personal vendetta for Liam. Denise could smell it on him; she just hadn't figured out what his angle was just yet.

They all released a breath. Lexxy knew if they were convicted of Carley's murder, not only would she never forgive herself, but she knew they would fry for it since she was a woman.

"In the murder of Dutch Hassle, we find all parties guilty of First-Degree murder."

Lexxy almost passed out, along with Denise and Sha. Junie, Ella Mae, and Jayla each reached up a row to grab them to keep them together. Lexxy let out a small shriek, catching Cocaine's attention. He turned around with pleading eyes, and he mouthed the words, "I love you," to her. Paul and Quentin followed suit, knowing this might be the last time they ever saw them in such an open proximity.

"In the predicate crimes, also known as the RICO, we find all parties guilty."

Lexxy's heart literally felt like it was about to stop beating, like her air and life support had been snatched from her. Even with a lesser sentence, they would be looking at some major time, and Roman, he was an old man. He didn't deserve to go to prison.

Judge Givens nodded his head and sat back in his chair, looking at everyone in the courtroom. Lexxy hoped he wasn't going to try any tricky shit considering he'd already taken the money.

"Roman Blackwood, I sentence you to life at Shady Pines Nursing Home, where you'll live out the rest of your days, how many ever you have left."

Ella Mae was hoping for this. She'd put her bid in with Joseph to try and get him that even if he couldn't get completely off. Shady Pines was a high security prison facility for old folks. Ella Mae could come and visit with him, sit with him, and she could even stay the night on the weekends. This was the perfect sentence for her, other than him actually coming home, but she knew the law wouldn't be so kind to her husband and grandsons.

"Cocaine, Paul, Quentin, and Juaqeen Blackwood,

over the course of this trial, I've seen your family come and support you, your children even have come and made a huge impact on all of us. Your spouses and girlfriends, and the remorse you've shown has been remarkable, and it's because of that that you won't serve the full sentences for these charges. Juaqeen Blackwood, I hereby sentence you to twenty years to be served at the Pikewood Men's prison. Cocaine, Paul, and Quentin Blackwood, I hereby sentence you to fifteen years each to also be served at the Pikewood Men's prison, effective immediately. Court is adjourned."

Judge Givens hit his gavel on his stand and proceeded to step down. Lexxy, Denise, Sha, Jayla, Ella Mae, and Junie all ran down to their men, kissing and hugging them, saying their goodbyes. Lexxy didn't mean for Cocaine to see her belly, but the dress she wore somehow got tucked into her panties, and her protruding belly was now showing.

Cocaine noticed right away, along with the rest of the family, and his eyes were now watery for a different reason.

"I'm sorry, Coco. I didn't think it was a good time to tell you. I'm so sorry, baby."

"Don't be, this is the best gift you could give me. Continue on with my legacy, Sexy Lexxy. I love you."

Lexxy grabbed Cocaine and kissed him long and hard, savoring the moment, where she would remember this forever, at least for the next fifteen years. Though she would be able to see him in between the time and hold his hand, she wouldn't be able to kiss him like this, not for quite some time. With no conjugal visits, it was going to be hard, pun intended, to control the way they were feeling, but Lexxy wouldn't dare step out on her man, not even for some dick because she wasn't stupid; she knew that just because Cocaine was gone, that didn't mean he didn't still have eyes and ears everywhere, and she wasn't that type. Fifteen years was no time when you were in love. Sure, it would be hard, but she would stick by his side no matter what.

Quentin held onto Sha as long as he could, until the guards pulled him away, and it was the same for all of them.

"Take care of my baby!" Jayla yelled to Juaqeen.

"I got you, baby. I love you, Jay!"

"I love you too, Qeen, forever."

Denise kissed Paul goodbye, and all of the men were carried away to the back. This was by far the worst day of all of their lives.

Roman, who had been biding his time for the last several months, knew and accepted his fate. He would be fine with going to prison forever, or not. He just didn't want to worry Ella Mae. He knew she'd been praying her britches off, and he just wanted to make sure that she was ok. If everything else went wrong, all he cared about was her.

After saying their goodbyes, they did the only thing they could do, was go home and all be together. They had a lot to do still. They needed to plan for Lexxy's baby that was just now being revealed, and they needed to stand by one another more so than ever before.

S everal days went by, and Denise had made up her mind. It didn't matter if it was in a church or in jail, she wanted to marry Paul, and she was going to no matter what. Since they'd finally been transferred to prison, they were allowed to do more than they were before and getting married was one of them.

Against Paul's wishes, Denise made him sign the papers. She threatened to leave him otherwise, which was almost what he wanted. He didn't want her waiting on him for that long. Though they'd get out early with good time, there wasn't enough "good time" in the world to end their sentence early enough. With all of their good time added up, as long as they got into NO trouble, they'd only serve eleven years, but that was still a long time. They'd all be a whole decade older. Cocaine's twins would be teenagers, and the new baby would be almost a preteen.

Denise was determined, and no matter what Paul said, they were doing this. He complained for two weeks straight about how he didn't want to do this. That she didn't need to feel forced to marry him, and she couldn't believe that because they were absolutely going to get married before this whole thing happened, and nothing was going to change that, not even a little prison sentence.

She finally got Paul to sign the papers and send them in, and they made an appointment for the following Monday for them to get married. Though Denise couldn't wear her wedding dress, nor could she invite her friends and family, she was just happy to be with her man and take his last name.

And even though they weren't technically allowed conjugal visits, they were able to pay the guard to look the other way for a few minutes so Paul could get it in with Denise. She hoped she would get pregnant so she would be able to have a little piece of him, but she didn't want to get her own hopes up.

The morning they were to be wed, Denise showed up at the prison an hour early to allot for any mishaps or bullshit that may or may not happen. She also wanted to give Paul time to get his nerves together, but she knew one thing, he better not leave her standing at the prison altar.

Finally, the time had come for her to become Mrs. Blackwood, and she halfway expected her father to bust through the prison doors and ruin this time too, but she got lucky; there were no signs of her father. It was just her, the Chaplin, the guards, and Paul.

She stood there with nothing but the rings they were promising to one another. The ceremony wasn't going to be romantic, it might not have even been sanitary, but that didn't matter.

"We are gathered here today to join Denise Ellis and

Paul Blackwood in marriage. Did you all prepare your own vows?"

"No offense, homie, but we gangstas, and gangstas don't need vows. She know how I feel about her, and I know how she feel about me, ain't that right, baby?" Paul asked. In all honesty, as badly as he wanted to marry Denise, all he could think about was getting into her guts.

"I understand," the Chaplin said in a hurry. He had been told about the agreement the couple had with the guard prior to coming in the room. He was told to keep it short, sweet, and to the point.

Several seconds later, the couple was saying yes to their nuptials, rings were exchanged, and they were on their way to handle their business. They'd only have about ten minutes, but Paul really only needed three. He had a strong nut waiting to bust inside of Denise, and he didn't care if she was bent over or if she was riding him. He had somewhere to put his kids, and as long as it was inside of Denise, he didn't give a damn.

The guard let the Chaplin out of the room, and he locked it behind him. He got on his walkie talkie and told his buddy in the AV room to cut the cameras for twelve minutes. They would have ten minutes to handle business and two minutes to get cleaned up.

The guard turned his back and placed his headphones in his ears. He didn't want to hear what was possibly about to happen. This wouldn't be the first time he'd done this kind of thing. Honestly, he was happy to do it for people. He could only imagine how he would feel if he were in this situation, and he hoped somebody would do the same for him, even though he might not have the same amount of money to pay for such privacy.

After he slipped in his headphones, he started the timer for exactly twelve minutes. Paul pulled his pants down, and Denise felt like a little girl, like a shy virgin.

"Baby, what's up? We ain't got time for you to be actin' all shy and shit. Bend that shit over and bust it open for me."

Denise had tears in her eyes, and this was not the time for her to be doing all of this.

Paul climbed up on the table, and he brought Denise into his arms, and he held her for a moment, kissing her on the neck, which allowed her to loosen up a bit.

"Baby, calm down. I know this ain't how we envisioned it, but that don't matter. We together, and you're my wife. You're Mrs. Paul Blackwood, you know, on some white people shit."

Denise knew he was right, but she couldn't bring herself to stop crying, and Paul wasn't going to fuck her like this. He stopped kissing on her and pushed her away from him lightly.

"We don't have to…."

Before Paul could say another word, Denise put her finger up to his lips, and she dropped down to her knees. She was feeling all types of crazy. Her emotions were all over the damn place, but she wanted to please her man and get everything she came for.

They only had eight minutes left, so she was going to have to suck his dick as fast as she could and then pop her pussy for him.

Her mouth was wet with saliva, and for a minute or

two, Paul was going in and out of her mouth, trying to feel her tonsils. Suddenly, he started to feel like he couldn't take it anymore, and he didn't want to cum in her mouth, he was aiming straight for the uterus. He pulled her face away from his dick, and it made a pop sound like a suction cup. Denise pulled down her leggings and her panties and bent over. Her pussy was wet just from sucking his dick. She loved the way Paul reacted to anything she did to him. He always acted like it was the best he ever had, and to him, it was. Paul loved Denise so much, any bitch he'd known or even met before that wasn't shit compared to her.

When Denise bent over, her pink pussy shown its pretty, wet face. She just looked like she was ready to get fucked. Paul slid in with ease, and as soon as he got inside, he thought he was going to lose it. They only had four minutes left, and for three of those minutes, he went wild, stroking her as hard as she could, so hard, she was falling over. She had to grab on to the table for stability.

"Paul, cum inside me, now!" she yelled.

He didn't need to hear anything else. Hell, he didn't even need to hear that because his eyes were rolling in the back of his head before she even said that, but hearing it just made it that much better.

His sexual eruption flowed into Denise's womb, and she'd already cum twice. The guard yelled "One minute," and they began scrambling to put their clothes back in order. Denise planted one last kiss on him, and then they sat down at the table to have their "reception." Since they were married, the warden allowed them to have a few extra hours together than most people got in their visits, which was perfect because now Denise really didn't want to leave.

"You think we can pay him again?" Denise asked.

"Shit, I don't know if I can go again, baby. That shit almost just took me out."

Paul and Denise both laughed, and they spent the rest of their day together, enjoying their union.

Though it may not have been conventional, they were just happy to be together, in love, and married.

Back at home, Sha received a text from Denise letting her know that she and Paul were married, and she couldn't have been happier, but a part of her was jealous. Since the trial, Quentin hadn't called her not once. He wasn't writing to her, no nothing. He had no communication with her at all. When Paul called to talk to Denise, she'd often ask for him to put Quentin on the phone, and he wouldn't come at all.

Sha had spent the last several days crying herself to sleep. Without the physical presence of her love, she thought she would crumble, but now, he was completely ignoring her and not talking to her at all? That was the lowest blow of all.

It was around four o'clock, and the mail man was in her yard. She usually met him at the mail box and waited for a letter from Quentin, even though he'd only sent two letters the entire time he'd been locked up, but she hoped that since he wasn't calling, he'd send her something.

Sha opened the door and peeked outside toward the mailbox.

"Anything for me today, John?"

John, their normal mailman thumbed through the mail and pulled out several things for Sha. She didn't really care about the bills; what she wanted to know was if she had anything from Quentin.

Sha snatched the envelopes from his hand and ran into the house. As she went through the mail, she threw down anything that didn't have Quentin's name on it, which was everything until she got to the very end, where she found what she'd been looking for.

On the top was Quentin's name along with his TDOC number, and it even smelled like him. Lawd, what was she going to do?

She ripped the letter open, trying to read it in a hurry, hoping everything was ok.

"Sha,

You know I love you and shit, but I ain't like my brother; falling in love wasn't easy for me, and the shit still ain't easy, and all I can think about is you waitin' on me for the next eleven years. Ma, your whole life will be gone. You'll be almost in your mid-thirties, and I can't do that to you, baby. You deserve somebody who can be there every day, who you don't have to worry coming home to you or not, or some sudden death type shit. I don't want that for you. I don't want you to think I don't love you because you for real, for real, my only reason for breathing. I love you so much, and it's killing me to leave you, but

I gotta do it because if I don't, you never will. But look, in eleven years, if you ain't got nobody, I definitely won't have nobody, then we can revisit this, but I ain't gon' let you wait around and love a ghost for most of your life."

There was no epic closing, nothing to hope for, nothing to look forward to. The letter ended abruptly, and she thought her life was over. Everyone around her had love and happiness, and here she was, miserable and depressed, but she told Quentin before she wasn't going to let him push her away, and she meant that still. She loved him with everything in her, and there was nothing he could do even if he thought he could, to push her away or make her leave.

Sha went upstairs to their bedroom and pulled out a pen and paper and began writing him back. She let him know that this was the last time she was going to have this conversation with him, and the only way out of this was death, and she meant that with all of her heart.

Sha wrote her soul out on that paper, and she eventually fell asleep with her pen in one hand and Quentin's letter in another.

After months of searching and plenty of money spent, Lexxy finally found Raul, and even though the boys were locked up and had been sentenced, he still had to pay for his betrayal. Lexxy was now eight months pregnant, and she shouldn't have been doing anything, but Lexxy was going to get revenge on all the people who were responsible for taking her family down.

Lexxy wanted to tell Sha and Denise what she was going to do, but she didn't want to bring anyone else into this mess if she didn't have to. It was bad enough that she was going at it alone, but it wouldn't be too hard. Even though Raul was a snitch, she didn't peg him for a killer. Any nigga who was weak enough to snitch on some niggas but wouldn't tell on the bitches, that said a lot about his character, and she was going to use that to her full advantage.

Lexxy hired a private investigator to find him, and he was held up at a hotel right outside of Nashville about an hour east. Lexxy had her gun on her, ready to let it loose on his ass.

All this time, she felt like she'd waited entirely too long to let something happen, to take control over her life, and this was it. Losing Cocaine to the system for the next eleven years would ruin her children, and she didn't know how she was going to tell Alexiana and CJ, and the new baby she was carrying when they got older that their father was a drug dealing murderer, but Lexxy put that in the back of her mind as she hit the highway to finish something that shouldn't have even begun.

An hour or so later, Lexxy found the hotel he was staying in, and she knew exactly what to do to get him to open the door. Raul was sort of stupid; his lack of common sense would be his ultimate downfall.

With her car parked a few spaces away from the door, she stood to the side of his room and knocked on the door. Paranoia seeped out of the creases of the room, and Lexxy laughed at herself. This nigga was probably on the run from everyone, so of course he was afraid and flinching at every knock, sound, and anyone who looked at him a little too long.

"Who is it?" Raul asked as he looked out the window, but Lexxy was on the opposite side of the door, so he couldn't see her.

"Yes sir, I'm here to change your sheets and bring you new towels."

"Oh, come in."

That was his biggest mistake.

Raul opened the door and tried shutting it just as quickly when he saw Lexxy's face, but she pulled her gun out of the jacket she had on and forced her way into the room.

"Lexxy, what—what are you doing here?"

"Good question, Raul. Have a seat."

Raul did exactly as he was told. He was more bitch made than Lexxy thought.

Though she was feeling like a complete thug, she needed to make sure her baby was safe, so even if she wanted to put her gun away to have a civilized conversation, she couldn't.

As he sat in the chair in the hotel room, he thought about all that he'd done wrong, and he knew Lexxy had come to serve him justice.

"Just kill me, Lexxy. I deserve the death of a betrayer. I did the one thing you should never do; I'm sorry."

"Not so quick. I'm not takin' you up out outta here until I know why; you got some serious explaining to do."

Raul shook his head and thought about his options. He was going to die either way, but he might as well die having redeemed himself because he was never going to get another opportunity like this.

"I didn't want nothin' to do with this; I really didn't, but it was Dutch though. He was in cahoots with that fed dude, Liam. He was paying him off all these years to stay off of him and to stay off of you, and that was cool and all until after he died, the money stopped coming, and I guess that pissed him off, but Liam had me watching y'all, all the time. He said they were going to hurt my family if I didn't do it. You know I got kids, Lexxy, what else was I supposed to do?"

"You were supposed to say yes and then tell us. We could've protected you and your family. We would've made sure y'all were safe. You know that."

"At the time, I didn't think so. The shit was just

happening way too fast, and I didn't really know what to do—I didn't."

Lexxy thought about it, and this still wasn't adding up. Why would a stickler like Liam allow Dutch to go free, to get away with all the things he'd done? Because compared to Cocaine, well to really of them, Dutch was still the person who was much, much worse.

"I still don't understand. Why would Liam be taking bribe money? That makes no sense. Why would he want to protect Dutch, to protect me, I guess I should say? Is it about Denise? Was he trying to protect Denise?"

"Liam is a weird ass dude, Lexxy. He'll say one thing in one breath, and another thing in another, but the truth is, he's ruled by love. I'm guessin' before this bitch he's dating now, there was no other woman, but the woman he's dating now got him so on lock, he'll do anything she tells him to do."

"A woman?"

In all of the time she'd known Liam, she'd never seen or heard about him being with anyone. Even when she and Denise were teenagers, that nigga seemed like he mainly stayed to himself, so what could he possibly be talking about?

"Yes, a woman. Most niggas, when they love their woman, will do anything for them. You should know that, Lexxy. Look at Cocaine. He's taking a charge for you that most people don't even know about, and that charge is what really put this shit into full effect."

"Wait, what do you mean? You talkin' 'bout 'cuz I killed Carley? How does that have anything to do with any of this?"

"Dutch wasn't as stupid as y'all thought. Liam had me follow y'all that day to take pictures of what went down. Dutch called Liam before he even left the house and let him know that if some shit went sideways, he had something to deliver, and that something was me. When y'all killed Dutch, that was like pulling the trigger of a gun that had already been drawn. Liam's woman is Carley's mom. He'd been able to keep her cool for a little while, but not forever. She was the one who turned your ass in. She didn't think Liam was getting the job done fast enough, so she took matters into her own hands and went over him. Why you think he's going so far? That nigga was mad offended when his own woman took his shit to the feds that are higher up than him. The only way to save his job and his relationship was turn everybody in. Carley's mama, Bianca, wants y'all head on a platter."

"And do you know where Bianca is?"

Raul put his head down. He didn't want to get anyone else hurt. He just wanted to clear his conscience before he went up out of here, but if he told Lexxy where Bianca was, then she was sure to die.

"I don't know if I should tell you that, Lexxy. I don't know."

"You gon' die anyway, might as well get it all out of your mind so you can go on to the upper room or to hell empty, no thoughts, no look backs, no regrets."

Raul went to reach for the paper on the nightstand, but Lexxy didn't know that was what he was doing, so she shot him in the arm once.

"Damn it! I was just tryna get some paper."

"You should've said something, Raul. Get the paper and write down that bitch's address."

With his good arm, he swung around and wrote down the address on the paper, and he dropped the pen back on the nightstand.

Raul knew his time had come, that he couldn't hide anymore. He was going to meet his maker. He just hoped that his children never knew about his traitorous ways. He prayed that nobody treated them differently because of his actions. In hindsight, it all made sense. He wasn't really built for this game. Every time Raul had to carry out an order, he felt like he was killing his community, and that wasn't who he was; he wanted to be a part of building it back up, but he couldn't do that without a little money. Something that started out as a plan to help his community, eventually turned into a game that there was only one way out of, and this was it.

Raul cried; if getting shot in the arm was what it was going to feel like when she shot him again, because she was going to shoot him again, then he wasn't ready for it, and even though he wanted to be strong in this moment, he didn't have a strong muscle or bone in his body. He felt like the weak, yellow bellied scum that he was.

Although Raul snitched on them, Lexxy didn't have malice in her heart for him. She was mad at him, but in a way, she felt sorry for him. There was no telling what she'd do if her family was at stake. In fact, it was the love of her family that was driving her to bring Raul to meet his ultimate fate.

"Close your eyes, Raul, and pray. Pray out loud."

"Our Father, who art in heaven,

Hallowed be thy name;
Thy Kingdom come,
Thy will be done on earth as it is in Heaven.
Give us this day our daily bread; and forgive us our trespasses
as we forgive those who trespass against us; and lead us not into
temptation, but deliver us from evil
For Thy is the kingdom, the power, and the wisdom,
Ame—

Lexxy pulled the trigger, releasing one bullet into his skull. She hoped for his soul's sake that that prayer somehow saved him. Lexxy wished she would have done this sooner, but this murder would've damaged the boys' case even more, and she wouldn't be the one to jeopardize it for them.

Lexxy left that room still feeling terrible. Something wasn't sitting well with her. If Bianca wanted justice or some type of revenge, why hadn't she come after her? Why was she directly going after the boys? Perhaps, she figured to take away the people they loved the most since Carley had been murdered.

Unfortunately, Lexxy knew what it was like to lose a child, at the hands of Bianca's daughter, Carley, so she could only imagine how she felt, but she deserved it. Carley was like a wild dog that had to be put down, and Lexxy just happened to be the one to do it.

With this new information, Lexxy figured it was just a matter of time before Bianca would be coming for her, so she needed to get ready, as ready as she could be anyway.

Lexxy had to get home so she could tell the girls about what happened. She needed to let them know what was really up because things were probably about to get a lot worse. It didn't seem like they could before this, but now, they most definitely were.

It was starting to get late, and the sun had long gone down. It was after seven p.m, and she knew Denise and Sha would worry if she took too much longer to get home.

Using Siri, she sent Denise a text letting her know she'd be home soon, and that there was still so much to discuss.

Siri confirmed the message, and then sent it. As Lexxy was at a stoplight, she heard the music in the neighboring car, and it was a song she could never forget.

"It ain't nothin' for me to ball on you,

It ain't nothin' for me to spoile ya',

If I adore you…."

It was DJ Khaled featuring Nicki Minaj and Future *"I wanna be with you."*

She remembered once for her and Cocaine's fourth anniversary, he had packages delivered all day with clothes, shoes, flowers, bundles, all types of shit, and he just kept singing that song to her the entire day. Now that he wasn't here to spoil her, she didn't care about the money, the clothes, the cars, none of it. It didn't mean shit without him.

The light turned red, and she found herself humming the song to herself and even rapping Nicki's part even after the car that was initially played it pulled away.

Lexxy was singing so loud, that she didn't feel or hear the pop that happened in her stomach when she pulled off, at least she didn't know about it until she got to the next stop light. Out of nowhere, she started feeling like she was going to explode, like her back might give up on her.

"Oh no, not right now, baby." She rubbed her belly as she continued to drive. She was nowhere near the hospital she planned on giving birth at, but she couldn't wait. She had to get to the hospital.

Siri came through with the rescue. Lexxy told Siri to call Denise, and she did it quickly.

"Hey, sis, where you at?"

"I'm…on my way…to the hospital…baby…now!"

"Ok, ok, calm down. Which one?"

"Vandy. Get my stuff and come on."

"On my way!"

Denise hopped off the phone and started moving around the house like Speedy Gonzalez. She was glad that she was already at Lexxy's so she could get her the things she needed. Denise grabbed her hospital bag, and Sha was already in the car waiting for them to leave so they could meet the newest edition of the Blackwood family.

<hr>

When Lexxy arrived at the hospital, she pulled up in the front and left her car running. She didn't give a damn about that car right now. For now, she just wanted to make sure her baby had a safe delivery. She was leaking amniotic fluid everywhere. Her bag didn't just break, it was punctured, so it was like she was peeing all over herself.

"Ma'am, yes, I'm in labor. My contractions are three minutes apart—" Lexxy almost collapsed, but luckily, a nurse saw her when she came in, and she whipped a wheelchair around like she was driving for Nascar.

"Yes, ok, and do you have anyone with you who can fill out your paperwork?"

"No, it's ok, I can do it, slowly."

The charge nurse handed Lexxy the clipboard and paper and they rushed her to the back. This baby was not going to wait.

Surprisingly, Lexxy was able to fill out all the paperwork. She had done this before, so it wasn't that strange, and even though she was in the pain of her life, she still felt ok for a woman who was in labor, as ok as she could be, because really, a part of her had gone numb.

Lexxy gave the nurse her paperwork, they got her up on the table to get her an epidural—she couldn't wait for the drugs, and they would be starting momentarily.

They waited a little while for the epidural to kick in, and when it numbed her all over, and she finally felt like her baby wasn't ripping at her insides, she was able to calm down, and follow the instructions the doctor was trying to give her.

Lexxy didn't want to have the baby without someone being in the room, but it didn't look like Sha and Denise were going to make it in time, and the doctor said they couldn't wait any longer.

"Come on, Lexxy, come on. You've got this. Push!"

Lexxy began trying her best to push, to get the baby out of her, but her mind wasn't in it, and she was numb, so the pain was gone. She wished she could hold this baby in for the next eleven years so she didn't have to have her baby alone, so that her baby wouldn't have to grow up without a father.

Wild Bill, Junie, Jayla, Ella Mae, and the kids were on the way, but Lexxy didn't know that. Denise had called them all on the way over. In that moment, all she could think about was how alone she was. Her husband was in prison and none of her family was here with her.

"Come on, Lexxy, you've gotta push!"

Tears slid from the sides of Lexxy's eyes. She knew she needed to push, but she couldn't will herself to do so. After everything that had taken place, Lexxy just wanted to die on that table. She hated the way she felt right now. She was miserable inside, and without Cocaine to cheer her up and bring her out of it, what was she going to do?

A few seconds later, the delivery room door burst open, and in walked Sha and Denise, fully scrubbed up, ready to be there for her.

"I know you didn't think you were having this baby without us!" Denise said as she kissed Lexxy's forehead.

Sha went around the other side of the bed and held her hand. "You can do this, come on."

Lexxy hadn't had the urge or even the want to push until she saw the girls. Though Cocaine wasn't there with her then, he was always in her heart, and she just needed a little reminder of that.

"Come on, Lex, you got this. You can do this. I've seen you go through so much worse. I know you're hurting because Cocaine isn't here. I know you'd rather have him in here with you than us, but one day, and I promise, one day, we gon' all be together again, but now, you gotta push. You gotta have this baby. You understand me?" Denise asked, and Lexxy nodded her head. Denise always had a way of getting Lexxy together when she needed to.

Lexxy, hearing Denise's words decided to push. She would never do anything to purposely endanger her baby's life, but she wasn't thinking. Her heart ached for her man, but she was going to do this and make him proud, make him remember why he loved her so much, not that he needed a reminder because he loved Lexxy with everything inside of him.

"I see the head, come on, Lexxy, keep pushing."

Lexxy pushed and pushed until there was nothing left to push. She didn't want to know the sex of the baby until it came out, but she did have some names planned for when the baby arrived, none in which she'd discussed with Cocaine.

When the doctor pulled the baby out, he looked up at Lexxy and asked, "Did you want a boy, or a girl?"

"I just want a healthy baby, doc."

"Good, but it's a boy," he said as he laughed and passed the baby to the nurse to have its nose suctioned and do a precleaning.

"Another boy? Oh lord, what are we gon' do with all these Blackwood men?" Sha asked, giggling.

When the nurse came back over and handed her the baby, he was so handsome, but not as chocolate as Alexiana and CJ, but still beautiful. He looked more like Jayla than Juaqeen or Cocaine. He had her eyes, and even her lips. He had Lexxy's ears and a full head of hair like she did.

"Hello, baby. I think I'll name you….William Leon Blackwood."

Lexxy looked up at Denise and Sha who were both nodding their heads yes. She named her baby after her father and the man who helped raise her husband. Without Wild Bill and Leon, there was no telling where either of them would be right now.

***

"Look, there he is, there he is right there. Say hi, brother," Jayla said to Alexiana and CJ who were thrilled by the fact that their mother was having a baby. They'd been the babies for so long, they couldn't wait to play with it, but Jayla explained that babies were fragile, and they couldn't be played with right away, but they were no less in love with him.

Ella Mae, Wild Bill, Jayla, and Junie stood in front of the nursery, wondering how Lexxy was doing. A nurse was coming to get baby William to take him to Lexxy, and they were finally about to see her and get to hold the baby, if she would let them.

Each of them had to wash their hands of course before touching the baby.

"I just want to kiss him!" Alexiana screamed when she saw him in the same room as her.

"Me too, Mommy. Can we kiss our baby brother?"

"No, not yet. Babies can get baby acne on their faces. They're little red bumps, and we don't want that happening to your baby brother, right?"

"Right!" they both yelled. They were both being so good about this, Lexxy was shocked and in amazement.

Wild Bill came over to the bed and kissed Lexxy on the cheek, and then he looked at his grandson.

"Well damn, Lexxy, this baby looks like Jayla."

Jayla smiled, as she knew the baby did.

"He does, doesn't he? He's beautiful, just like his grandmother."

Jayla blushed. She was getting all the praise.

"Listen, I got something for you," Wild Bill said as he took his phone out.

"What is it, Daddy?" Even though Lexxy was a grown woman, she still loved presents from her father.

Wild Bill held his finger up, and he pressed the Facetime button on his phone, something he'd recently learned to use.

The camera came on, and Wild Bill took the baby and handed Lexxy the phone.

"Hey mama, you did good!"

Lexxy's hand flew to her mouth. As she lived and breathed, Cocaine, Paul, Juaqeen, and Quentin were all in the camera. She just wished that Roman could have been there, or at least seen this moment since he was a great grandfather, again, but he was in Shady Pines, still living it up. Money went a long way there, and Roman's money was long like the Nile River.

"Bring the baby back over here, let him see him," Lexxy said as she cried.

Wild Bill brought the baby back over and put him in the camera.

"What did you name him?"

"William Leon, a name befitting a king."

"I couldn't agree more, baby. You ok?"

"Am I ok? I'm more than ok. When did you get a phone?"

"That's a real long story that don't even matter right now. We had the money to get one, so we got one, but I ain't been callin' you from it for just in case, baby."

"I need to tell you something, Coco. All of you. GG, can you take the kids out of the room?" Lexxy asked Ella Mae who was more than happy to take the babies outside where they couldn't hear whatever was about to come out of Lexxy's mouth.

Lexxy went on to tell them about what she'd done and how this was all going to play out. Lexxy of course wasn't going to be able to do anything because she just had a baby, but that didn't mean that Sha and Denise couldn't.

"And if y'all do that, baby, y'all gon' have to get ghost, if y'all can pull it off."

"It ain't a question of if we can pull it off, how we gon' leave afterwards?" Sha asked from behind the bed. She was looking directly into the camera at Quentin, who though he was trying to avoid her, couldn't help but stare into her eyes. He truly loved her; he was just childish. He was afraid to really let someone love him and for himself to love anyone else.

"Let me talk to Roman and see what we can come up with. He might know some shit. Hold on, baby, I'ma pass the phone around. You know they wanna see the baby too. They some old soft ass niggas."

Lexxy giggled as they passed the phone around, taking screenshot pictures of them with the baby in the camera and Lexxy too. Denise and Sha both got to have a few moments with Quentin and Paul, and Quentin apologized for acting like a jack ass and told Sha he loved her.

Her night couldn't have been more complete. The stress she was feeling for her strained relationship had almost become too much, so for them to make amends, it changed her whole life, at least for now.

"I love you, baby. I'ma call you later tonight to check on you, ok?"

Lexxy didn't want him to go. She was seeing him and loving it, and she didn't want his voice or his face to be out of her sight or earshot.

"Come on, baby. I promise I'ma call you tonight. I

love you. I gotta make some moves so we can see about gettin' y'all up out of here, ok?"

Lexxy nodded her head, trying to hold her tears in. She didn't want Cocaine to see her crying.

"I love you. I'ma hit you later."

Cocaine kissed her through the phone, and then he hung up.

While she was lying in bed, she wondered if she would really leave just to save herself? Was that something she was truly willing to do? She couldn't really say; but if Denise and Sha were going to do what she thought they were, they would have no choice but to go on and leave the boys behind.

everal weeks passed by, and Denise and Sha had planned to get to Carley's mom's house and kill the bitch. Denise also hoped her father was there because she would probably kill him too. A monster like that couldn't be allowed to live because with all the information he knew, he could finish wrecking their lives for good, and they'd all be behind bars.

Lexxy went home with baby William, and Denise and Sha went to handle their business with Bianca.

"Don't do nothin' stupid. Be smart. I don't know if y'all should be going alone."

"Yes, we should. We can't just let this shit go. We gotta put down all of our enemies, even if it means we gotta do it alone. I've never been afraid to put in the work, I just never had to before," Sha said, making sure they all knew what it was.

"Well, I guess it's a good thing I got the kids' passports then, huh? Is this really happening? Once we do this, there's no turning back."

"We know. Call Roman. Tell him to have the chopper ready for us in three hours. If we don't make it back…"

"Denise, shut up! Ain't no if you don't make it back.

I'm not leaving without y'all. We're in this together. I'm about to call Roman, now y'all go on and handle your business. Be careful, and I love y'all."

Lexxy, Sha, and Denise embraced one another before they left the house.

Lexxy had no clue if they'd even make it back alive because this was truly a suicide mission.

They were stepping into dangerous territory, so she could only hope for the best, but the best wasn't always what was to come.

Alexiana and CJ had been staying at Wild Bill and Junie's the last few weeks so that Lexxy could get settled with the baby, but now it was time for them to come home so they could all be together with Wild Bill, Junie, Ella Mae, and Jayla one last time.

She sent Wild Bill a text telling him to come on over because if things played out the way she thought they would, there would be no more time; they'd have to just go.

Bianca's house was just about forty minutes away, which was perfect for them because they were going to need time to carry this whole thing out, and neither of them knew how it was going to go down or if it was going to happen at all.

When they got to the house, Liam was standing outside, kissing on Bianca, necking with her like they were a bunch of teenagers. This was the perfect way to get them, but neither of the girls were sure of their shots. They didn't know if shooting them would be that easy, then that would give them a chance to get away, so they instead parked the car and figured they'd come up on them by food.

Sha went around the back from one of the other neighbor's houses so no matter what, this would turn out ok. With Denise in the front with a gun, and Sha in the back with a knife, their plan was to make Liam surrender any of his weapons right then and there and then lead them into the car, where it would look like a murder suicide.

Sha knew how autopsies worked. They would see the endorphins released into Bianca's brain that she would be releasing from the fear of being killed.

Stealthily, Denise walked up behind her father with her gun pointed toward his head.

"Liam, drop whatever weapons you got on you, and that phone can go too."

Bianca's eyes lit up in horror. Was this really happening in her neighborhood? Were they about to be robbed?

Liam turned around and saw Denise's face plain as day. She wasn't trying to hide it or cover it up; there would be no witnesses left here today anyway.

It was close to ten-thirty, no reason why they shouldn't be in the house. Shit, they were asking to be killed, clearly.

"Denise, is that you?"

"You know it's me, or have you forgotten what your own daughter looks like? I wouldn't be surprised—"

"Ah, ah, ah, bitch, don't you move," Sha said as she snuck up behind Bianca, putting the knife to her throat. "Put that phone down, now, bitch."

Bianca had reached her hand into her pocket to try and dial 911, but Sha was quicker than that, and she had been watching the whole time.

"So, what's your plan here? You willing to kill your father over a hoodlum? I raised you, what happened to you?"

"You happened to me, you lying sack of shit. When were you going to tell me you had a girlfriend, better yet, when were you going to tell me it was Carley's mom? Isn't this some type of conflict of interest? This has to be against some type of rules."

"Denise, you haven't been a part of my life for some time now, but that doesn't matter, baby. We can fix this; it doesn't have to be this way."

Liam began inching his way toward Denise, and she started coming closer to him.

"Liam, get in the car, you too, bitch," Denise said as the true killer inside of her began coming out.

Sha and Denise led them to the inside of the car, and she stood there staring at her father.

"You know what'll happen if you kill a federal agent, don't you? You'll go to prison for the rest of your life, they might even have your head, baby. Is that what you want?"

"I'm not worried about it either way. You took my life

the day you ruined my wedding. I still got married, by the way!"

Denise wiggled her ring finger at her father, showing him that she was still happy and still had the man of her dreams.

"And just so you know, Bi-an-ca…" Denise purposely broke the syllables to her name down for dramatic effect. "Your daughter beat Lexxy's baby out of her, so that's why your daughter was done in like that. Your daughter wasn't killed because she was a good person or because of some street beef. It was all because she took Lexxy's baby from her, so she did the same thing. She killed Carley as payback. Meanwhile, y'all shackin' up together, one of you is probably using the other one, if not both. Tell me, Dad, you and Bianca been together long?"

Sha just stayed in place. She knew Denise needed to get this off of her, especially if she was going to end up killing her father tonight.

"Answer me, damn it!" Denise yelled.

Sha looked around to make sure no one saw her, and so far, everything seemed to still be at peace.

"Five years, we've been together five years," Liam said, trembling.

"Interesting. You all must've gotten together around that time, huh? The time that Carley died?"

Liam had never honestly thought about it before. It never seemed suspect to him, but now that Denise was saying it, it did kind of seem bad.

"Bianca, was this…was it all just a set up?"

Bianca dropped her head. She loved Liam, but she didn't always. She got with him out of spite, to try and bring down the Blackwood family. Quentin and Paul had made it clear to her what happened, and she wanted to take the whole family down, so she got in touch with Liam, saying she had information, which she did, and then, slowly, they fell in love with one another, and of course, there was nothing in this world Liam wouldn't do for his beloved Bianca, even if that meant ruining his own daughter's life because he'd lost her long ago.

"I'm so, so sorry, Liam. Truly, I'm sorry."

"And there you have it. You let pussy fuck your life up, man, that's ok because you're about to fix it. We'll always be looking over our shoulders if you don't die, Liam, and I won't live like that, and I damn sure won't have my family living like that. Give me the knife, Sha-Sha."

Sha slid the knife over to Denise. "Here, slit her throat. I'm not gon' do it, you are."

Liam looked at Denise with shock and confusion on his face. "Yeah, slit her throat, Liam. This is both of your faults, so y'all gon' die by each other's hands because really, that's what happened. You gon' slit her throat, and then you gon' kill yourself, and if you don't, I'ma shoot you both."

Sha was surprised at how gangsta Denise was being, especially with her own father. It took guts to kill your parents, but if she was going to do it, Sha would wholeheartedly support her.

"I'm not going to kill Bianca, Denise. You might as well kill us bo—"

Denise was tired of hearing him talk, so she did what

he asked. Time was running out, and they still needed to get back to get their things and their money.

Denise pulled the trigger, four times. She shot Bianca once in the head, but Liam, she almost couldn't stop. She shot him three times because she was angry, and she was sick of his shit. He was the reason that her happy ending had been taken from her over and over again. Not just now, but even as a child. He'd been setting her up her whole life, and now, it was time he felt how she did.

Liam and Bianca would have just kept coming for them if they didn't kill them. They were the ones who cared most about this case before it got the attention of anyone else.

"You got the stuff?" Denise asked Sha.

"Yep."

Sha was carrying around a small can of lighter fluid in her pocket, along with a lighter. She dowsed the car with lighter fluid, and then, they started walking away. When they were far enough away that they wouldn't be hit by the aftershock of the car blowing back on them, Sha tossed an open lighter onto the car, and Bianca and Liam's body burned like barbecue.

"You know there's no looking back now, right?"

"I know. Ain't nothin' to look back to," Sha agreed.

They got into their car and went to the house they shared with their men and got the things they held dear to them along with their money. They went ahead and ditched their phones, not knowing if they would soon be being tracked. Besides, if they were being tracked, when they left, their phones would still be at home, and they'd be gone.

They didn't have much money at home since they'd left it at Wild Bill's, who was bringing over as much cash as he could carry in the trunk for them, which was a lot considering he was driving an SUV.

Denise wished she could feel bad about the fate that fell upon her father, but it was his damn fault, and he deserved everything he got, even the death he got.

Sha did a quick sweep of the house, making sure they had everything they needed, and they headed out, never to see that house ever again.

As soon as Wild Bill arrived, he loaded up Lexxy's car. The plan was in full motion, and they were all saying their goodbyes. Lexxy shared one final Facetime with her man, the last time she'd see his face in God knows how long.

"Hey, beautiful, you all set? I talked to Roman, and he's got everything waiting for you."

"Yeah, we're ready. I just wanted to call you and say—"

"Don't say goodbye, baby, it'll never be goodbye. When this time is up, I'ma come and find you, baby, I promise."

"How will we keep in touch? It won't be safe for us to have phones, at least not to be calling each other."

"We'll figure it out, baby. You got lil' man's passport?"

"Yeah, Joseph was able to help us get it rushed. I've got everything. Cocaine, I'm scared."

This was something he'd never heard Lexxy really say before, but then again, this was the first time they'd ever been apart.

"I know, but you gotta do this. I ain't mad for what Sha and Denise did. They made the same call we would've made, baby. It's gon' be ok. Now y'all go ahead and do what you gotta do. Keep your head up, baby. You was made for this shit. You strong like a diamond, you ain't gon' crumble under the pressure."

Lexxy had snot and tears running down her face, but she had to go because she had other things she needed to get.

Lexxy gave the phone to Denise and then she gave the phone to Sha, and they all wished each other well.

Quentin and Sha officially made up, and he promised when he came home, he wasn't gon' still be kickin' that same shit about not wanting to be together anymore, that no matter what, they would end up together.

As Lexxy's family sat in the living room, she looked at all of them with love and fear in her eyes.

"Look, you gotta go, baby girl. Don't worry about us, we gon' all be ok. We all too old to run anyway. Besides, we gotta stay here and make sure the boys are on the up and up."

"But what if I never see you again, if we never talk again?"

Junie stepped forward and wrapped her arms around her daughter. "As long as we got breath in our bodies, there will always be time for us to talk and make the impossible happen. Now y'all gotta go, please. I want y'all to make it. Take care of my grand babies, ok?"

Lexxy nodded her head, and she continued getting her and the children's things together. This was not easy. This was even harder than watching the boys be locked away.

How was she supposed to move forward without her man? How in the hell were they going to get out of this one?

Thankfully, Lexxy thought to get CJ and Alexiana passports when they were babies, and with the help of Joseph, she was able to get William one too. If their only hope was getting out of the country, they would all leave immediately.

Jayla and Ella Mae decided to stay behind. They'd said they were too old to run, and the feds didn't have anything on them anyway, so they were scot free.

Lexxy decided they wouldn't pack anything unless it was of sentimental value. They didn't need anything. They had plenty of cash, so money wasn't an issue. Lexxy's only fear was the fact that she had an infant that she'd be traveling with, and she didn't want to get caught trying to leave the country with them.

Roman had arranged a private jet for them to leave as soon as they were ready, which was now.

"Mommy, where are we going?" Alexiana asked Lexxy as she grabbed her hand, tugging on it to get her attention.

"We're going on a vacation. It's going to be so much fun."

"Without Daddy?"

Alexiana was a true daddy's baby, and Lexxy hated

that she had to leave Cocaine behind, but she had to keep her children safe, and they couldn't lose both of their parents. There was just no way she'd allow that to happen.

"Yes baby, but one day, your daddy will come back to us. I promise."

"Pinky promise?"

"I double pinky promise. I love you. Now go downstairs and wait for Mommy with Auntie Sha and Auntie Denise."

Alexiana went downstairs and joined her aunts where CJ and baby William were already waiting for them.

The only thing Lexxy wanted to take with her were a few of Cocaine's clothes and some of their pictures since she'd have to ditch yet another phone.

She collected the pictures, took one last look at the house, and they left.

The private jet that would be taking them to the Galápagos Islands was waiting for them. The three women had their doubts about leaving their lives behind, but what choice did they have? The feds were on their trail, and if they didn't leave now, there would be no escaping.

Together, they boarded the jet and flew off into their new destiny. Lexxy didn't know how she'd be able to get word to Cocaine, if she'd even be able to. The phones weren't safe, even with a burner phone, she didn't trust it. If she sent him a letter, they could be watching his mail. All Lexxy could do was hope that when the time was right, she would be reunited with the man of her dreams, heart, and soul.

Sha and Denise were optimistic. They'd managed to keep a clear head the entire time they were getting ready for this giant move. But on the inside, they were crumbling with fear. They told themselves that everything would be ok and the time would fly by, but they didn't know that for sure; it just sounded good.

<hr>

Seven years later....

"Alexiana, CJ, William, get up! Y'all gotta get to school. Come on now, don't embarrass me!"

Lexxy's children came stumbling down the stairs of the beautiful three-story mansion she shared with Denise and Sha. The last seven years had been hard and troublesome. Trying to stay hidden in a wanted world was not easy, even when you weren't in the country that wanted you.

They were able to use their real identities although Joseph was able to send them fake ones. Lexxy figured it was easier to hide out in plain sight, at least that's what Cocaine had told her. The only communication she had with him was through Joseph, and she wasn't even able to speak with him for long for fear of the feds tracking his phone and movements as well. Seven years was a long time to go without being able to hear your significant other's voice, especially today.

Lexxy had been up all-night tossing and turning, sleep refusing to settle in. Today was Cocaine's birthday, his thirty-eighth to be exact.

Every year, Lexxy still celebrated his birthday, as they all celebrated for their men in their absences.

Alexiana and CJ knew why their mother was sad and why she seemed a little more irritable today than usual. She hardly ever yelled at them, but this morning, she was barking orders at them left and right. It was like no matter what they did, they just weren't moving fast enough. William was just seven years old, and he had no clue why his mother was that grouchy, but it made him no never mind; he just went on about his business as usual.

"Here, sit down and eat breakfast," Sha said as she brought food to the table for everyone to eat. "PJ, stop playing with your fork and put it down, wait until the food actually finishes getting to the table!"

"Yes, Auntie Sha-Sha," PJ agreed.

Denise indeed got pregnant that day she had sloppy sex with her man, and she gave birth to Paul Jr on the islands.

Denise and Lexxy came downstairs with the children rushing past them to get to the table.

"Slow down!" Denise yelled as she slowly came down the stairs. It was a rough morning for all of them because they all mourned the memories of leaving their lives behind, not separately but together.

Alexiana, CJ, and William dug right into their food, not leaving even a crumb on their plates.

"I guess I'm raising savages. Come on, let's get y'all out of here. PJ, you bring your behind on here too before you miss the bus."

PJ took one last bite of his pancake and grabbed his backpack.

"No goodbye kiss for mama?" Denise asked, half-jokingly.

"Sorry, Mom." PJ leaned over and kissed Denise, hugged Sha, and ran for the door.

"Y'all got everything, right?"

Lexxy inspected the kids making sure they had everything they needed for the day. It was something about Mondays that really fucked with the kids' brains.

When she was satisfied and knew they had everything, she opened the door to let them run out to the bus stop so they wouldn't miss it. Every morning, Lexxy waited at the door to make sure the kids got on safely. The world was a dangerous place, and they'd fought too hard to let anything bad happen to their children now.

Lexxy closed the door and she went to the table to enjoy her breakfast.

"You ready for your mimosa?" Sha asked as she poured their drinks.

"You better know it! To the greatest man I've ever known, happy birthday, Cocaine!"

They clinked their glasses and drank to Cocaine's birthday. As they sat at the table, it was quiet, each of them reminiscing on the moments they had with Cocaine, Paul, and Quentin, and it never got easier, never. Time only made it worse.

Suddenly, there was a knock on their door. It wasn't uncommon for people to knock on their door. They had very friendly neighbors, and they were all rich. Lexxy went to the door, and it was indeed one of her neighbors.

"Mrs. Ethel, good morning. What can I do you for?" Mrs. Ethel was an older Hispanic woman who knew all the neighborhood gossip, and she assumed she was coming over to tell her some, which she didn't mind. She liked knowing who lived around her for just in case.

"I came to invite you and the girls to my house tonight for a party. I figured when you didn't RSVP you must have not received the invitations in the first place. Seven o'clock sharp. I'm celebrating my fiftieth wedding anniversary, and you girls have been so kind to me, me and Morty would love it if you were there."

As bad as Lexxy wanted to stay home and cry, she couldn't refuse this sincere invitation.

"Of course, we'll be there."

Lexxy hugged Mrs. Ethel and proceeded to close the door when a familiar scent hit her nose. This wasn't uncommon, she thought she smelled Cocaine all the time, but she knew that was just her senses playing an evil trick on her. The door was closing behind her as she walked away, but the door never closed, so she turned back around, and before she could fully turn around, Sha yelled out.

"Oh, my fucking God!"

Lexxy wasn't sure what kind of face Sha was making, and she didn't know what to make of Denise's face either.

"What's the matter with y'all?" Lexxy asked.

Sha and Denise's index fingers went up, and Lexxy finished turning in the direction they were pointing in.

"Sexy Lexxy, what I tell you about locking doors, baby?"

Right in front of her was her man, her king, her world, in the flesh. She couldn't believe it. There was no way this was happening. He came closer to her where she was frozen in place. He touched her cheek with his rough, chocolate hands, letting her know this was really happening.

She looked into his beautiful brown eyes, and it was too much for her. Lexxy collapsed on the ground right in front of them.

"Oh Lord!" Sha said as she ran in the direction of Lexxy. She shook her, trying to wake her up, and then, she smacked the shit out of her, knowing that would bring her ass back.

The smack was so loud, Jesus had to have heard it as it echoed off the walls of the house. Lexxy jumped up and looked around, and there he was, still staring at her.

"You ok, baby?"

Lexxy felt like a small child. All she wanted was to be in his arms again. Lexxy took off running and jumped on him, wrapping her arms and legs around him like a spider monkey, crying like a small child.

"Shhh...I know, I know baby. It's ok. Shhh..."

Cocaine did his best to quiet her cries, but he was unsuccessful.

"How? Tell me how!"

"Well hold up woman, while you demandin' shit."

Cocaine went back to the door and opened it back up, and Paul and Quentin appeared from behind the door.

Sha wrapped her arms around herself, and Denise couldn't stand being that far away but still so close to her man. All of them embraced one another, swapping hugs and kisses.

"How is this possible, baby?" Lexxy asked once more.

"It took us seven years, but we found someone to help us shawshank our way the fuck up outta there. The same nigga that helped Denise and Paul with their twelve minutes of pleasure, yeah, we all knew about that. We paid off some of the guards to sneak us into the old part of the jail and let us go. The alarms went off the moment we got down there. The fat fuck, well, the one who really didn't want to help us but didn't have no choice in the matter, didn't wanna lose his job I guess, baby, but when them alarms went off, I knew it was time for us to get the fuck up outta there, and we didn't waste no time. We ran, straight to Joseph's house. When we got there, he fed us, gave us these tacky ass clothes, and thanks to g-daddy, we were able to get out just in time."

"What about Juaqeen? Is he ok? How long y'all been havin' this plan? Did Joseph know?"

"He's good. He said he was gon' stay. He wasn't goin' nowhere without moms. You know that. Joseph knew everything, but he couldn't tell you. If it didn't work, I didn't want you to be disappointed."

Lexxy couldn't believe this. Was her family really and truly finally done with the running? Could they all live happily ever after?

The three couples sat at the table talking and catching up on what they missed together, and they vowed that no matter what, they'd always be strong, always be together, and no matter what, they'd always be a family.

Cocaine grabbed Lexxy by the hand and took her out onto the balcony of the second floor, a place he'd become acquainted with in the last few hours.

Lexxy stood in front of him, looking out over the ocean with her fingers laced in his as his arms were wrapped around her waist.

"I love you, Alexxus, and I ain't gon' ever let you go, baby."

"Please don't, hold me tighter."

Cocaine held Lexxy as tightly as he could. They stood on the balcony together until their legs got tired, and then they went into their bedroom where they rekindled their sweet love all day.

Neither of them knew what the future held, but finally, they were together, and that was all that mattered.

Cocaine could resume being a father, truly get to know his children, and be the husband he'd always been, even from far away.

Quentin, Paul, Denise, and Sha spent the rest of the day, doing the same, loving on one another, promising each other to never let the other go, and all was at peace in the world.

When the children came home, they were just as happy to see their fathers as their mothers were.

Cocaine knew he had a lot of restorative work to put in, but he didn't mind. This was his life, his legacy, and he was thankful in this moment to be the thug ass nigga he'd always been or else he would've cracked and lost his mind.

But you know what they say, All the Fine Ass Dopemen have done it better than anyone else, and that couldn't be truer in this case....and they all lived happily ever after 🤍

Did I mention this isn't the end of the story?...

I wrote this series seven years ago, and to this day, I use it as a bar to see how far I've come. I always say, "I want this to be as good as Cocaine and Lexxy," or "I want to feel as good as I did when I wrote Cocaine and Lexxy."

Cocaine and Lexxy hasn't only become a part of your lives, nor is it just a chance to try my work out. It truly became my livelihood, and at one point in time, and even now, I feel and have felt as though I owe this series everything.

Please, leave a review. Be looking for the spin off as well later. This book hasn't been changed, just revised, and I hope it's even better than you remember if this is your second, third, or one hundredth time reading it. If this is your first time, I hope the series has been good to you. Thank you for the love and support. I'm truly thankful.

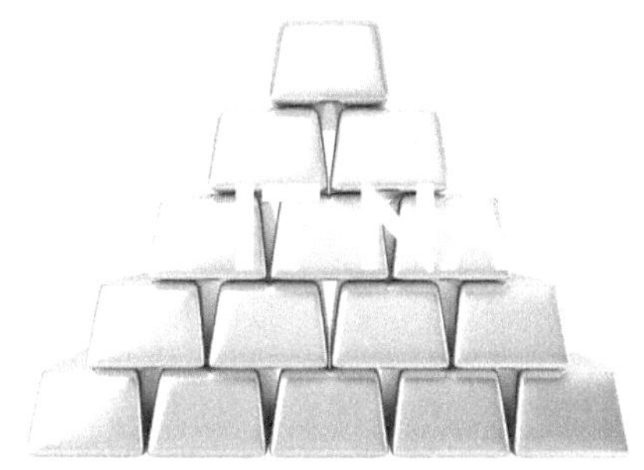